CRUEL PROMISE

MIKA LANE

HEADLANDS PUBLISHING

COPYRIGHT

BE THE FIRST TO KNOW…

Want more heat, heart,
and bad boys who know what they're doing?
Join my list and I'll send the steam straight to your inbox,
starting with a deliciously naughty story:

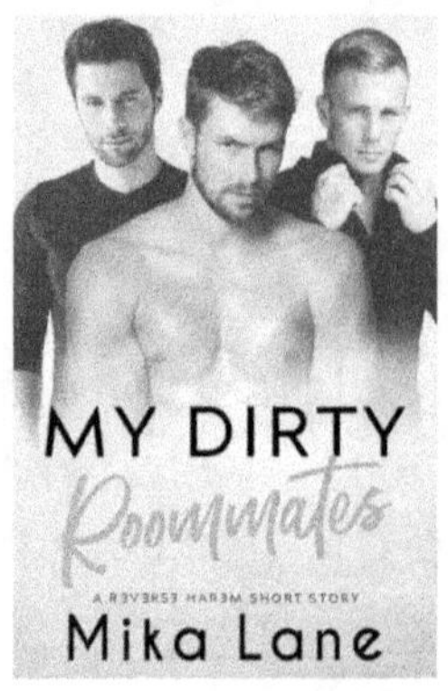

SIGN UP TO MY MAILING LIST!
Or visit:
https://geni.us/free-book-signup

PROLOGUE

I knew those bastards would show up.

It's not enough that my parents are dead, burned to crisps in a house fire that flamed so fast and hot they couldn't even reach their bedroom door.

It's not enough that my Uncle Mikey—formerly Misha, before he fooled himself into believing people would think he was American with a more Anglo-sounding name—is gloating in the corner, face wet with crocodile tears, counting the money he'll make taking over my father's club. And his wife in a brand-new fur coat even though it's too warm outside for a light jacket.

Nor is it enough that the two shots of whiskey I threw back to help me get through the day are churning in my stomach like toxic sludge.

To make matters even shittier, the Yegorov faction had to show up, as if they care that my parents are in closed coffins because they're burned so badly they can't be put on display. As if they're mourning that the head of their biggest rival faction—the one led by my father—is now dead. As if they give a shit about expressing their condolences to my brothers and me.

They're having their best day of the year on what is undoubtedly the worst of mine.

My parents deserve to be honored today, not surrounded by a bunch of greedy, gloating bastards.

Hell, Papa was not my favorite person. He was volatile and selfish. And my poor mother put up with more of his shit than any woman should have to.

And then there were the mistresses, one of whom is making her way through the receiving line toward my brothers and me, rivers of thick, black mascara running down her fake tan face.

All faults aside, he was still my fucking Papa.

"Told you they'd show up," Kir says, not bothering to lower his voice.

The receiving line, a hideous formality the funeral director recommended, twists out of the room, the end nowhere in sight, leaving my brothers and me to robotically shake hands with the throngs of people who've come to pay their respects.

I have no doubt most of them owed my father money and are stopping by only to ensure he really is dead.

I'm half-tempted to open his coffin so these fuckers can see his charred remains.

Yup, he's dead, folks. But that doesn't mean your debts are released.

"Oh, Vadik. I'm so very sorry."

I'm eye-to-eye with the manager of Papa's club, Dominika Federova, a 'friend' from the old country who came to the US around the same time my parents did.

A coincidence?

Hell no.

When he was alive, Papa never admitted Dominika was anything to him aside from his formidable club manager—and I will give the woman that much—she's always run things with an iron fist. But it would take a fucking idiot to not see there was more there.

But, as much as she would have liked to, for all the years she was his mistress, Dominika was never able to displace my mother, a Mrs. Grigory Alekseev. She might have fucked my father six ways from Sunday, but it was never enough to drive a wedge between him and his *real* wife—Mama. That's because, in our world, marriages are business transactions. And Mama's family connections are what helped my parents come to the US and finance Papa's rise to the top of our Bratva faction. In fact, if he had lived long enough, he would have become the *Pakhan*. Not that he wanted to be that high up in the organization. He was quite happy managing the day-to-day in his own local faction.

That was Papa. Ambitious, but not enough to make enemies.

Or so we thought.

While Dominika never had a chance at becoming Papa's wife, she was given the opportunity to have a career. To make money. Which was probably better for her, in the long run.

After all, if she'd been in bed with Papa the night of the fire, she'd be lying in the coffin right next to his.

"Nice of you to come, Dominika."

She wipes her tears, smearing more mascara across her cheeks. Why do Russian women of her generation wear so goddamn much makeup?

"Vadik," she says, lowering her voice and moving closer to my ear, "what... what will become of the club?"

Fuck all. She's no different than anyone else here.

Looking out for herself, and damn the Alekseev brothers who are burying their parents.

I steady my voice to temper the explosion simmering behind my insincere smile. "Dominika, all that will be settled soon. Today is not the day."

Her head snaps back at what she no doubt perceives as a slight. She's always been temperamental. Hell, if I were the one in charge, I'd have fired her ass years ago just to get her out of my face. But Papa was loyal. He knew a good worker when he saw one. And a good lay.

But it's clear that today, more than anything, Dominika has her livelihood on her mind. Not her dead lover.

I suppose I'd want to know my future too. Guess I don't blame her for that. But at the fucking funeral? She can't wait a few days?

She can piss right off.

To let her know she's dismissed, I turn to the next person in line, a little weasel of a man who always tried to be part of Papa's social circle, but for a variety of reasons, remained on the sidelines. This man, I know, owes Papa money. Not as much as some others, but if he doesn't watch himself, he'll fall into a pit of debt from which he'll never recover. He's heading for trouble, and is here to ingratiate himself to my brothers and me.

However, that's not my problem. He's a grown man and needs to handle his own shit.

"I'm so very sorry about your father, Vadik. He was a good man," he says.

I shake his clammy hand. "Thank you, Mr. Gates. I appreciate that."

"I… I…," he stumbles.

Is he actually going to try to talk business too? I'm so over these insincere assholes.

"Not the time, Mr. Gates," I interrupt, and look at the receiving line, the end of which was still nowhere in sight.

God help me.

But one thing does catch my eye. Standing near the doorway, alone, with her back to the wall, is a young woman in a slim black dress and scuffed shoes. Her hair is in a long brown braid pulled over her right shoulder, and she's looking down as if she actually appreciates the solemnity of the occasion. She might be the only person here who does.

As if she can sense my gaze, she looks up at me, her plump red lips a contrast to her milky white complexion. For a moment it's as if there is no one else in the room. Everything gets quiet—the low murmurs, the sniffles, the glad-handing.

She tries to look away out of respect for my grief, unlike the other jokers and looky-loos who are glad my old man is dead, but she doesn't. Her head tilts the tiniest bit, and for a moment, I want to take her hand and lead her out of the funeral home, away from the hypocrisy and self-interest surrounding me, and pretend it's just another day where my rage is under control and I'm not dreaming of taking a machine gun and emptying this room of all the assholes in it.

As if our connection is too intense, she gasps, bringing her hand to her mouth. She turns and runs out of the room, and the noise surrounding me returns, that of a funeral for two murdered people.

My parents.

CHAPTER ONE

Two years later

CHARLEIGH

There my father was, in a spreading pool of blood. I look around the pawn shop. Where had the kid trying out the trombone gone? The one making so much racket I had to duck into the bathroom to continue a conversation with my big sister, Lily?

She wants me to join her in New York with our youngest sister, Evie, and at this moment in time I wish more than anything I were there, or at least anywhere but here. Lily has a new boyfriend and a place for us to stay. She wants to get us away from Pops and the pawn shop, which she always says is a 'bad influence,' and 'no place for young women to grow up.' Exactly like my mother used to say.

I have no idea what Lily's doing for money, and how she can suddenly afford to support Evie and me in the very expensive borough of Manhattan. I don't ask.

I've never been to New York. Hell, I've never been out of Illinois. But I know about the Big Apple, thanks to the stories my Lily has regaled me with over the past couple years she's been there. Some are happy, some are not. But she loves it there and swears Evie and I would too.

I'm not so sure I believe her. And I'm not so sure she loves it as much as she claims. From what I can tell, it takes a certain kind of person to thrive in New York. And until now, until this new boyfriend came on the scene, I wouldn't say Lily was thriving all that well. She works like a dog and has to swipe food from the catering company she works with just to feed herself.

But she's in the middle of convincing me that things have changed for her, for the better, and she's ready to help. I can continue to work toward my bookkeeping certificate at one of the community colleges there, and Evie can enroll in a high school that's better than where she is right now. Lily says there are lots of good public schools in New York, and that with her new connections, she can get Evie into the best.

Easier said than done. Dragging Evie away from her friends, as dirt-baggy as they may be, will not be easy. And as for me, I've had so many things promised to me in my life that amounted to nothing more than a bunch of hot air, that I am more than cynical. People lie and promise shit all day long just to get what they want.

If it seems too good to be true, then it probably is.

That's what Pops always says. Someone brings him a heavy gold necklace or luxury watch, and is willing to let it go at a bargain-basement price, you can bet it's either stolen or fake. He says if anyone owned these items outright and knew their worth, they'd never pawn them for the pennies on the dollar they're willing to walk away with.

Yes, my father is careful who he deals with, having learned the hard way. He used to accept most anything that came his way, but after getting in trouble for it, he got more particular.

I know it bummed him out, because he made a lot of money off those things. He didn't care whether they'd been stolen. In fact, I think he still does fence stolen goods from time to time. He just keeps them hidden in the back, where the authorities are least likely to look.

What can I say. My father's ethics, or lack of them, seldom get in the way of his making a buck.

But they'd never caused him to be lying on the floor of the shop, bloody and moaning either.

"What's going on—" I start to say, Lily yelling the same in the background over our long-distance call.

"Charleigh?" she screams through the phone. "Charleigh—"

I squeeze my eyes shut and wish she were here. She always knows what to do. She always protected Evie and me. That's why she feels so guilty about leaving us to go to New York.

But before I can make sense of Pops's blood and respond to my sister, the phone is snatched right out of my hand.

CHAPTER TWO

CHARLEIGH

"Hey—" I yell, whipping around and attempting to grab the phone back before I even see who took it.

"Quiet," a voice growls.

I glance up to see a man with a crooked nose and shaved head. He looks familiar. His blue eyes narrow, and his lips press together tightly, reinforcing his stern expression. He's in control. Confident to the point of arrogance.

What the hell?

Do I know this guy? It seems impossible—how could our lives ever intersect? And yet, I swear I know his face.

I tear my gaze from the man to my bleeding father, and as if I were looking through a thick fog, I scan the shop trying to figure out what's going on. The strange thing is, I can barely see anything. I'm on the verge of a full-blown anxiety attack, my brain overloaded by my surroundings. Nothing makes sense. The kid who was trying out the trombone, whose racket sent me to escape to the bathroom, is nowhere to be seen. In his place are three men in suits, as if he has grown taller and multiplied.

Through the blur, I see the men are somber. Unsmiling. The kind you don't mess with.

You don't grow up around a pawn shop and not develop *some* street smarts.

As my vision clears, I realize they're staring at *me*.

These guys haven't happened by for a friendly *hello*. Or to sell something they found in their grandmother's basement, which they hope is worth more than most of the junk here.

These guys could be anybody. Pops does business with lots of people. Although I've never seen anyone hurt him.

I can guess they're not from the city or county government, come to check that Pops isn't selling stolen goods again. Those men don't dress nearly as nicely, nor are they as good looking as these three.

I might be frightened, but I still notice certain things.

Like these men, who look like they could grace the cover of *GQ*.

No, they're not here to sell or buy. I'm sure of that. Aside from their handsome but hard, stern faces, they wear the most perfect suits I've ever seen. Not a single wrinkle, crease, or fluff of lint to be found. Crisp white shirts and ties of thick, sturdy silk. Unscuffed black shoes.

People like this do not come to pawn shops.

Are they holding Pops up? Pawn shops keep lots of cash. I know this because many times over the years Pops has had me go to the bank to make a deposit. That is, a deposit of the cash he was willing to claim on his taxes. The rest of it goes in a safe in the back, hidden behind a false wall.

I don't understand…

The man who took my phone drops it into his suit pocket, amusement crossing his face when I hold my hand out for him to give it back.

He does not.

I raise my chin like I'm not afraid, but men like this see right through my false bravado. They smell fear. They thrive on it. They eat it for breakfast.

Pops continues to writhe, holding his head, although I'm not sure exactly where he is bleeding from. The thick, red goo continues to spread in slow motion over the shop floor, like a glossy halo.

"Honey, go back in the storage room. Just go wait there."

Victoria, my dad's one employee, gently takes me by the arm and tries to steer me out of the room. "C'mon, Charleigh. You don't need to see this."

She's always been kind to my sisters and me, trying to shelter us from the seedy side of pawn shop life, having worked here almost since Pops opened the place.

She especially tried to step up to the plate after my mother was murdered in a burglary. But my dad would only let her get so involved with us. Said she reminded him of our mother and he just could not bear that. In fact, at one point he was going to fire her. But my sisters and I begged him to let her stay.

As much as I know Victoria has my best interests in mind, I shake her off my arm to let her and the men know I'm not going anywhere.

"Pops, let me see your head," I say, kneeling at his side.

When I finally locate his wound, a large gash on the side of his head, my heart pounds double time, and I am woozy.

Dammit. This is not the time to be squeamish.

The men yell at Dad, and when he yells back at them, the blood pulses a little harder from his head. I start to see stars, so I sit on the floor next to him, pressing my hoodie to his injury.

I've heard head wounds bleed like crazy, but this is insane.

"What's going on, Pops?" I plead.

CHAPTER THREE

I am yanked to my feet before my father can answer.

"WHAT do you want?" I scream at the man who grabbed me, the one with his hair styled into a weird man bun.

Who is equally as handsome as the bald one who swiped my phone.

"This is none of your business," he says, looking at me so intently I am forced to look away for a moment.

I stretch up to my full height. I am tall, but still not tall enough to see this man eye-to-eye. So I look up at him because I have no choice. "Get off me, creep," I hiss, trying to shake him away.

To no avail.

Victoria on the other side of my father, arms crossed tightly, paces the floor. Does she know something?

She must.

The first man, the one who looks familiar, steps in front of me and tilts his head with a curious stare. "You sure have turned out to be quite the beauty."

Who *is* this person?

He turns to the others. "Guys, look how grown-up Gil Gates's daughter is now. How old are you, pretty girl? Eighteen? Nineteen?" he taunts.

"None of your fucking business—" I start to say.

"She's twenty, Vadik. Now leave her alone. Please," Pops says in a weak voice.

Vadik's eyes widen. "Damn. I thought when I saw you at my father's funeral two years ago you were jailbait for sure. Shit, you were eighteen. I could have hit on you if I didn't have all those losers sucking up my time, supposedly paying their respects."

I wince at his vulgar words and remember. I did see him that day at the funeral I went to with my dad. It was for a man he did business with and his wife, who both died in some sort of tragic accident. On the sign outside the funeral, the name was Alekseev, and there were tons and tons of people, far more than there were at my mother's funeral. And they were very dressed up, not simply, like my mother's friends were.

Pops told me the Alekseevs were from Russia. Guess the name stuck because I'd never heard a Russian name before.

"I do remember you. Your dad…" I trail off.

What am I doing, engaging with this man?

He lights up at my recognition and breaks into a grin. "Yup. Papa burned up in a house fire, along with Mama. Didn't he, boys?" he asks, looking at the other two men.

Who bear a slight resemblance to him.

Because they are brothers.

It's all coming back now.

What do they want from Pops? And what is this man doing speaking so cheerfully about his father's death? What is wrong with him?

"You're the Alekseevs then, right?" I give the guy holding my arm a dirty look.

"My head hurts," my father wails from the floor, distracting us all for a moment.

But only a moment. Seems these guys have done this before. "That we are, Miss Gates, the Alekseev brothers. I'm Vadik, the man on your arm is Kir, and that over there is Niko. The baby of the family."

I look at Niko to see how he receives this

acknowledgment. He just shakes his head with a small laugh.

"Why did you hurt my father? What do you want?" I demand. I want answers.

Yeah, right. Like I can force these men to do anything, much less answer a simple question.

Kir loosens his grip on my arm, not entirely letting go. "Why don't you tell your daughter what's going on, Mr. Gates? She deserves to know what kind of person you are."

Anger swells in me. My dad will never win any Father of the Year awards. But he *is* my dad. And I want to know what the hell is going on.

"Oh, honey," he groans, reaching for me, but just brushing the hem of my blue jeans. "I… I have some debts."

Vadik drops his head back with a loud roar. "*Some* debts, Mr. Gates? Sounds like you are down-playing the mess you are in, sir. Do we have to show you again just how much trouble you've gotten yourself into?"

Debts? Pops has debts? While we're pretty much middle-class, my father makes a modest living from the pawn shop and we're not wanting for the basics in life. I can't imagine why he's in debt.

And why these men care.

Unless…

I turn to him. "Pops, do you owe these men money?"

CHAPTER FOUR

Victoria continues her pacing, avoiding my gaze. Yup. She knows something.

And Pops, the blood around him turning dark and crusty since his bleeding has pretty much stopped, cowers under the menacing form of Vadik. From the floor, he nods slightly at first, and then with a bit more vigor. "I have… gambling debts, Charleigh. A lot of them. Debts I owe to these guys."

That can't be. I know Pops plays cards. Poker games of all kinds. But he plays friendly games with his buddies. Not for money. Not real money, anyway. Just change. Quarters, nickels, dimes. That sort of thing.

I look at the Alekseev brothers, who stare back with blank expressions. This must be business as usual for them. Just another day at the office, roughing up someone who got on their wrong side.

Bastards. Fury grows in me and I get ready to tell them off. But my tongue is tied.

Vadik's blue-eyed stare takes me right back to that moment in the funeral home where our eyes met. I didn't know anything about him. Hell, I still don't. But his penetrating stare, two years ago, shook me to my core. I inexplicably dreamt of him for weeks after that day. And his gaze today is no less intense. I tear myself away from his scrutiny as a protective measure. Like if I let him look at me for too long, I'll be under his spell. He'll gobble my soul alive, leaving me nothing but a shell.

I'm afraid he's already doing that.

How can I feel such a strange attraction to someone who's hurt my father? What kind of daughter am I?

But I have other, more important things to figure out right now.

"Pops? If you have debts, why don't you just pay them? You have money, right? Let's pay these men and get them off your back."

My father looks up at me from the floor, the blood dried to a muddy stain on his previously white shirt. He extends my hoodie toward me. I take it even though I plan to chuck it, first chance I get.

"Char," he says in a soft voice, "if I had the cash, I'd give it to them. For fuck's sake."

Oh.

I see. And, as much as I'd like, there's little I can do to help. Every cent I earn helping out in the pawn shop goes to my bookkeeping courses, where I hope to earn myself a certificate that will allow me a profession that's respectable. Like my sister in New York.

Where I'll sit behind a desk and get deli sand-wiches for lunch every day. Where I can buy a couple nice skirts and blouses at someplace other than Target, as well as the kind of trench coat I see the office girls wearing to work in the warmer Illi-nois months. They look so chic, with their high-heeled pumps, nice handbags, and glossy lipstick. They are important. They do important work. They go to meetings and they take notes.

I know all this because my instructor tells me this is how bookkeepers work. She says I'll never get rich, but I'll be comfortable.

Which is fine by me. I don't need a lot of money. Just enough to take occasional weekend trips to see a show in Chicago. Enjoy a nice dinner out. Buy my sisters the sort of birthday presents they deserve.

But until I finish my certificate, I have none of

these things. Which is okay, because I know if I work hard, I *will* have them.

This is no help to my father's situation, though.

"Hey!" I shout as the younger brother, Niko, takes a step toward my father. My sharp voice stops him in his tracks, and an amused expression washes over his face.

Like these guys give a crap what I think.

"Gates, you have twenty-four hours to come up with the money you owe us," he says softly in my dad's direction, like he doesn't want to be the heavy.

"No!" Dad wails. "I can't get it that fast. C'mon guys. I've known you for years. I was friends with your father."

Kir scoffs. "You sponged off my father, Gates. You were no friend of his."

Oh my god. That's why we were at that funeral. The one Pops didn't want to go to alone.

Ever since Mother died, he can't go to funerals by himself.

The brothers head toward the door with me right on their tail.

"Honey," Victoria says, reaching for my arm.

I brush right past her.

"Look. Gentlemen," I say, choking on the word, "can we work something out here? Like a payment plan?"

Vadik looks at me sadly. Fine, I don't know how this stuff works. But there are always multiple solutions to any problem.

Right?

"I… I will try to pay it. How much time can you give me?" I ask desperately.

The three of them laugh as they push the store's front door open, jingling the old bell I've been listening to all my life.

"Don't stand in the doorway, kid," Kir says, gesturing with his chin that I should get back in the store. "You don't want to attract attention."

But I decide to press my luck and ignore him. He wouldn't hit a girl, would he? "Wait. Look, it's clear he doesn't have the money. If he doesn't have it now, he won't have it in twenty-four hours. What will happen then?"

Vadik and Kir ignore me and walk to their car. Niko, the one who's more softspoken, turns to me.

"You'll see, Charleigh. You'll see in twenty-four hours."

CHAPTER FIVE

VADIK

How in the fuck did my uncle make such a mess of the club? The one my father slaved over for so many years?

The one Papa never should have left to his ne'er-do-well brother Misha. Or Mikey. Who couldn't run away from his Russian roots fast enough.

That should have been ample warning. The man didn't give a shit about his family, or any of our businesses.

It's been two years since the house fire, the one my parents died in. Murdered, I prefer to say, although it's never been proven. And it's taken Mikey exactly two years to drive my father's beloved, very profitable club straight into the ground.

And now I have to fix it. Not because Mikey wants me to. Not because he's even asked me for help, which I offered on more than one occasion. I should have just wrestled the company from his slimy hands, but out of some inexplicable loyalty to my father and the family as a whole, I stood back. Respected my father's last wishes to give his party boy younger brother a profession. Something he could be proud of.

And what did the fucker do?

Spent every last cent the club had on exotic cars for his lazy ass and tacky fur coats for his child-bride wife.

I am not even kidding.

He dragged her over from Russia when she was fourteen years old—something about a business transaction between her father and him—and popped her cherry seconds after she turned eighteen. How do I know this? He fucking bragged about it.

I guess I should at least give him credit for not being a child molester.

And now the fucker has fled the country, wanted by the Feds on tax evasion charges. Of course, he tried to clean out the coffers before he left, moving money to a variety of offshore accounts he could easily access from wherever he landed.

But on this, I got the last word. I was able to move some funds into an account he had no knowledge of, just before he left. I knew he was up to no good. He's never been smart enough to hide his real intentions.

So, with Mikey out of the way, my brothers and I are left with two choices. Either clean up the mess left behind or close the club's doors.

I suppose it would be easier to walk away. Tell all our employees to get new jobs somewhere else.

Including Dominika, our high-handed club manager. Who I'd like out of our lives anyway.

But fuck it, we decided. Papa would roll over in his grave if he knew the shape the club was in only two years after his death. My brothers and I will do right by him and breathe life back into the place if it's the last thing we do.

The multitude of other businesses we run are doing fine. They will prop up this venture for as long as needed. The only downside is that for now, I have to deal with the fucking migraine headache of a mess my dumbass uncle left me.

But I have ideas. Lots of ideas. The kind that can be very profitable. And they start with chasing down all the fuckers who owe us money.

We run card games. That's not all the club is about, but it's a true cash cow. And Uncle was very lenient about letting players borrow from the house. In fact, he let *a lot* of players borrow *a lot* from the house.

Mikey was too much of a pussy to ever cut anyone off.

Even Papa wasn't much for collecting the debts owed him. As long as operations ran smoothly, he didn't sweat things.

But now, the bills are due, so to speak.

Some of our players owe us piddling amounts. We're not bothering with them. But anyone who owes us ten-thousand dollars or more, we're going after.

That includes Gil Gates, local pawn shop owner. Gambling addict. And father to the beautiful Charleigh.

Who I've not been able to stop thinking about since we left her father's shitty little shop.

CHAPTER SIX

VADIK

Gates is not the worst of our debtors, not by a landslide. And in fact, in some ways he's a lucky man. Many who are indebted to us are lonely old losers. Card games are their only social outlet, the only time they get out of the house, aside from grocery shopping and cashing their social security checks.

But Gates, he has that daughter. The stunner with the long brown hair and legs for miles, who cares enough about him to actually try to stand up to my brothers and me.

I have to admit, her false bravado nearly made me laugh a couple times. But I tamped that shit down. If she wants to stick up for her father, more power to her. And she was cute as fuck while she did it.

In fact, I'd be a liar if I didn't admit when she narrowed her eyes at me and clenched her fists by her side, I didn't feel that familiar twitch in my balls. The one that reminds me it's been too long since I've had a pretty girl suck me off, and even longer since it was one who put on a tough-guy act.

God, I love that. Badass-acting women who are anything but.

While I doubt he appreciates it, Gates is a lucky bastard that he has someone to care about him. Actually, I hear he has three daughters, although I know nothing about the other two, except that one lives in New York and the other is a high school kid.

The way his daughter Charleigh—weird name for a girl, if you ask me—ran to his side when she saw him gushing blood was so very... touching. Of course, the bastard is lucky he didn't get himself into a mess like this back in the old country—Papa's old country, I should say— where warnings were much more severe than getting hit aside the head with the butt of a gun. No, the stories Papa used to share were much more gruesome, involving severed fingers and even limbs—shit like that—for offenses far less serious than Gates's.

But that was his old life. America is more 'civilized.'

Actually, civilized is not the right word. America is just not as lawless as Russia was back in the former Soviet days. For one, our *Pakhan* keeps the worst of the violence under control. Says he doesn't want to attract any more attention than absolutely necessary. We do our best to fly under the radar, leaving little or no trace of our activities, whenever we can.

That means Gates is lucky we didn't break any of his fingers. I know how painful it is—it's been done to me. But such drastic measures require trips to emergency rooms and the like—although I had to suffer through mine with no medical care—which draws attention like nothing else.

Our roughing him up was perfunctory, really, and nothing more. The poor bastard will never be able to pay up. We took a cursory look at his books and he barely makes ends meet with his shop, which is probably why he got into card games to begin with. Thought he could make a little extra cake, pay off some bills, maybe take his daughters out for a nice meal.

Look how that turned out.

He's as bad a business manager as my fucking uncle, only difference is that Mikey had the brains to flee the country, and Gates let himself be a sitting duck.

Seriously. How fucking hard is it to run a successful business? My brothers and me, with our hands in all sorts of entities not limited to moving weapons, providing security services, and hosting illegal gambling, manage to keep our books in the black. That doesn't mean what we do is easy. Hell, it's dangerous as fuck and we are on constant alert. But these men who drive their businesses into the ground mystify me.

I close the office door because I don't need anyone knowing my state of mind, take a seat at Papa's old desk, and drop my head into my hands, a migraine circling my head like a starving vulture. I have a fuck load on my mind right now and I need to keep my head on straight.

And for some godforsaken reason, I can't get that girl, Charleigh, off my mind. The way she took up for her father, all brave and shit. She didn't fool me, though. She didn't fool anyone, much less herself. But I give her major kudos for trying.

This makes me happy. Very happy. Because our dealings with Charleigh are far from over and I look forward to her company.

CHAPTER SEVEN

VADIK

I plan to get to know our pretty, long-legged friend. Because as much as she wants to help her old man, she can't touch his debt. Hell, from the looks of it, she can't even afford to replace her tattered Converse Chucks. Though it was sweet she offered to try and bail out her father. She's the kind of daughter any dad would be proud to have.

She smells so damn good, as I knew she would, like pure heaven, if you could bottle that shit. Not perfume-y at all, just clean and fresh and sweet like the most subtle fucking flower you ever smelled. Too bad she hangs out in that crappy little pawn shop.

The way she pulled her shoulders back when trying to stand up to us, thrusting her small breasts out as if they were her freaking armor or something, was about the most guileless thing I think I've ever seen.

I know her type. Not well, but I know it. Girls like Charleigh don't hang out with guys like my brothers and me. In fact, our paths seldom cross. We usually end up with the bad girls, the dirty girls, who don't care that we make our living doing illegal shit. They just want our money and the security that offers. They want to be with the guy with the most power so they can lord it over other women, their friends included. In return, they'll fuck us day and night—even our friends, if we ask them to—and put up with the boatload of shit women in our world are required to. As long as the money keeps flowing, they don't give a damn what they have to do.

But someone like Charleigh, she doesn't know what to do about a guy like me—an admittedly dangerous and scary prick. Given the choice, she'd run in the opposite direction, were she to confront me in a dark alley. I represent everything she's not. Everything that's dark and forbidding and treacherous about the world.

Everything existing in a man who would hurt her father.

And God bless the man. Or damn him to hell, depending on your perspective. Just as my brothers and I were leaving his dump of a shop, he called after us, *offering her*. Yeah, he fucking offered us his daughter. Maybe not in the way we might have liked. But he put it out there when he suggested that maybe we have some work for her. Something that pays better than her little job at the shop.

Seems the man might be smarter than I give him credit for. Or at least more resourceful

I'm sure he had in mind having her serve cocktails or some such in the game room. I'm not sure he knows much about what we do in the rest of the club. But he knows enough. And yet he still dangled her out there in front of us, like a piece of meat to a hungry pride of lions. He's seen enough beautiful women come and go in the club, for a variety of reasons, to know that his Charleigh would fit in just fine here.

Whether she wants to or not.

That fact, he does not give a shit about.

Given the work I do, I hang out with some scumbags. Hell, sometimes I'm a scumbag myself. But this man, Gil Gates, has taken that shit to a new low.

Offering his daughter. I have to say, even I am a little offended by that.

But not too offended.

"Hey."

I yank my head out of my hands and look up to see my brother Kir at the door.

"Got another migraine?" he asks, gesturing in my direction with a toss of his chin.

I run a hand over my smooth head, shaved bald by my barber that morning, as if that would relieve the tightening belt around my brain. "I'm fine. What's up, Kir?"

I lean back in Papa's chair—even if it had been Mikey's for two years, I'll never call any of this his— and crack my knuckles.

My brother makes himself at home opposite my desk. "How are the numbers looking?" he asks. "Mikey's numbers?"

I shake my head. It's not worth being angry anymore. Waste of my energy. It's time to look forward.

"Well," I start, "I met with the accountant, and he confirmed that Mikey pretty much used the place as his personal ATM machine."

Kir scoffs. "Tell me something I don't already know. I swear, if I could get my hands around that fucker's neck—"

But I wave him off. I'm tired of the 'ifs.' It's time to deal with the situation. Not dwell in the past no matter how infuriating it is.

"We can get out of this, Kir. We can pull cash

from the other businesses as long as we need to. We'll collect what we're owed, pay off the debts Mikey racked up, and have the place back to Papa's standards in no time."

"What about the girl?"

Charleigh.

Fuck. I knew he was going to bring her up.

I choose my words carefully. My brother doesn't need to know I've spent the better part of a day thinking about the lovely lady.

"She… she can help us. She *will* help us."

A shit-eating grin makes its way across my brother's face.

Am I conflicted? Am I ever conflicted? For fuck's sake, am I pussy-whipped by a woman I don't even know? Who I saw from a distance at my father's funeral two years ago, and who I just saw for fifteen minutes as I gave her father a warning beat-down?

What the fuck is wrong with me?

Kir shrugs. "I saw how you looked at her. Better keep it together, my brother."

Bastard. That's the problem working with family. They know you too well. They can anticipate your next move. Your next words. Your next thoughts.

Push your buttons and all that shit.

I ignore my brother. Hell, I saw him checking her out, too. But I'm not saying anything. Not yet. "What does her father know about the club? Aside from the card rooms?" I ask.

"Vadik, he knows everything. How do you think he got his lame ass into so much debt? By sitting in the back of the room like a good little boy? He's up to his eyeballs in this place. Paying the strippers for lap dances, hiring out the hookers for a good time. The man ain't no saint."

That makes it all the more sordid, his willingness to pimp out his daughter.

Not that that changes anything. But as much as I've been around, I can still be shocked by the decisions people make from time to time.

Blows my motherfucking mind, this one does.

CHAPTER EIGHT

VADIK

I lift a paperweight from Papa's desk, a gift my mother got him on one of their working vacations, a trip to Italy to meet with the brotherhood there. In the yellowed glass there is a replica of the Leaning Tower of Pisa. It's funny, that such a clichéd little thing brought him so much happiness.

I roll the cold glass in my hands and, for about the tenth time that day, wish the old bastard were still around.

"He's throwing his daughter to the wolves," I say, stating the obvious.

Kir nods slowly, scrutinizing me. I wish he would back the fuck off. "You got concerns about that?"

I rub my temples again before I answer. "Nope. We got business to attend to."

"Vadik. Is this going to be an issue for us?" Kir asks.

I won't dignify his pain in the ass interrogation. I get to my feet. "C'mon. Let's get a drink."

He claps me on the back on the way to the door. "Now that's my big brother."

And that's my *middle* brother. The only way to change the subject is to mention alcohol.

"Dominika!" I holler as we settle into the dark, paneled-wall lounge.

I sink deeply into a crackly leather chair, and the scent of everything I remember from my childhood rises up to meet me—lemon oil on the furniture, cigars, and expensive whisky. I loved coming to the club when I was a kid. All three of us did.

Of course, Mama only let us come in the off-hours, when there were no girls running around half naked, and no grown men crying because they'd bet their house on a card game.

"Vadik. Kir," Dominika says a little over-solic-itously.

It's not like her to suck up. But she's nervous. If the club closes, she has nowhere to go. Hell, she's still bitter my father didn't leave her a red cent in his will.

Shitty treatment of a long-time mistress, but I have no doubt he had his reasons.

"Couple scotches, please," Kir says.

I watch Dominika disappear behind the bar, choosing the top shelf brand she knows my brothers and I prefer.

She brings us two Baccarat crystal rocks glasses, Kir's with ice and mine without. I suck down the liquor in one long draw. The migraine that was threatening was finally taking its leave thanks to the pain pills my doctor prescribed. Pills that are not supposed to be taken with alcohol.

But there are times I'll do anything to make the pain go away. Kind of like how Gil Gates will do anything to get my brothers and me off his back.

CHAPTER NINE

CHARLEIGH

"What's wrong with you today?"

Ugh. I thought I was hiding my distraction.

Dammit.

I think carefully before I speak. Luci's not only my study-buddy, but she's also become my best friend. Actually, she's my only friend. The last thing I want to do is lie to her, but how can I tell her about my father's debts, and the visit by those horrible men?

Who, if they're true to their word and return twenty-four hours after they first threatened and beat Pops, are due back at the pawn shop around five p.m. I will be there when they are. I don't have a plan yet, but I've been trying to come up with one.

So far, no luck.

Thus, the distraction that's so obvious to Luci.

"I… I'm sorry. Guess I'm not all here. My dad… is having some health problems."

That's not a total lie. I mean, he was bleeding all over the shop floor. I would call that a health problem.

Thank God my younger sister wasn't around to witness the mess, and in fact I've arranged for Evie to stay over at her best friend's house tonight just to ensure she stays away from the shop. I'm not particularly thrilled with the mom of Evie's friend—I have a feeling she gives them run of the house and anywhere else they want to go—but at least there's safety in numbers and they are clear across town. There's no way they'll pop in on my dad.

"What's wrong with your father?" Luci asks, frowning.

She knows a bit about my 'situation,' that since my mother died, my sisters and I were pretty much left on our own. Pops's employee Victoria picked up whatever slack she could, but when my older sister left for New York, all the responsibility for looking after Evie shifted to me. Not that I mind. It's just that my dad withdrew into himself after we lost Mother, barely getting himself out of bed to get to the shop every day, never mind taking care of his three young daughters. So, we figured stuff out on our own. It wasn't too hard.

Evie says Pops feels guilty, an interesting observation for someone so young. But I don't know what he should feel guilty about. It's not his fault Mother was at the wrong place at the wrong time.

"Pops… well, he hurt his head. He hit it on something. In the shop. Something hard. He was bleeding all over. You should have seen it. What a mess," I babble, the words coming more easily the more I say.

And to think I'm still not *exactly* lying.

A 'sin of omission,' my faithful mother would have called it. Yes, she did try hard to instill her church values in her daughters. But all that pretty much flew out the window when she died.

Was murdered, actually. It's still hard to say that. The 'm' word. So, I usually don't.

"Damn, girl, I'm sorry to hear that. Is he gonna be okay?" Luci asks, her face covered in concern that makes me feel like shit for sort-of lying.

I nod quickly. Probably too quickly to be convincing. "Oh, yes. You know, it's just… worrisome. All the blood that comes from a head wound is just crazy. It was scary."

Scary? It was freaking terrifying. And I'm afraid the worst is yet to come.

Luci extends her hand to mine. "That sucks. I'm so sorry. But look, we have an exam coming up. We're at the top of the class. We're gonna ace this one, Char."

She's right. The teacher, who's taken a liking to the two of us—she says she's never seen anyone work so hard in her bookkeeping class—gets to recommend her top students to the school's placement center.

That means jobs. And money. And no more scraping by with the minimum-wage pay Pops gives me for the few hours I help him in the shop. Of course, I can't move out of our apartment yet, not until Evie graduates from high school. But I can establish my independence and get some money in the bank for when the time is right.

There's a lot riding on this prize our teacher is dangling before us. And now, I have to worry about this business with Pops.

He wasn't a great dad before Mother died. I think that's partially why she turned to religion. Helped her get through the long days of parenting three daughters pretty much on her own. And after she was gone, well, he was more disengaged than ever.

But hell, he's my father, and I'll help him any way I can. Although maybe I should think hard before I say that.

Luci's looking at me like she can read my mind. God, I hope she can't, but we have a lot in common, with our religious upbringing, hardships, and other stuff.

"Is there anything I can do?" she asks.

And now the tears come. Dammit. The last thing I want is to let her know how messed-up Pops's situation is. Why make her worry? It's not like she can do anything to help, much as she might like to.

"Thanks so much, Luci. I really appreciate it. It's just been… a lot, you know. A lot with staying on top of school, keeping Evie out of trouble, and now my dad."

She nods. "Hang in there, honey. You'll come out on top. I know you will. When it comes down to it, we have no other choice."

She's right. There is no other choice for people like us.

CHAPTER TEN

CHARLEIGH

I pull into the dumpy strip mall where Pops's pawn shop is. All the other businesses—two nail salons, a laundromat, and a shady-looking tax preparation service—are dark, long since having closed up for the day. My father's is the only one with lights still on, the last beacon of commerce in this sad little shopping center, with its weedy, pothole-filled parking lot.

I park my beater car next to his. Victoria must be gone for the day. My car is a hand-me-down from him, really a piece of crap vehicle that was considered a beater when *he* got it several years ago. The car he's driving right now isn't much better, but a good couple months in the shop last Christmas season left him with enough extra cash for a long-overdue upgrade.

So, the beater was passed down to me, and I was thrilled about it. The fact that it just keeps running and running with minimal effort on my part—gas and oil changes, of course—is something my mother would have called a miracle. Proof that 'someone' out there is looking out for me.

At one time I might have believed that. Now, I call it dumb luck.

At this hour of the early evening, Pops's business is usually closed up too. He's typically tinkering in the back of the store with whatever merchandise came in that day or doing a little light accounting. Since I've been working on my bookkeeping certification, I offered to help him with this task. But he won't hear of it.

Which I think is strange. I guess he has his reasons.

Since the shop is closed for the day, there should be no other cars in the lot aside from ours. And yet there is one in the far corner, parked in the shadows. It's too dark to identify its make and model, but I am pretty sure it's black or at least a dark blue or grey. It's nice. Not like mine and Pops's.

I pray that doesn't mean what I'm afraid it might.

I knock on the shop's door and my father

answers it in an instant, letting me in and locking it back up behind me. While I give him a kiss on the cheek, avoiding the side of his head that was bleeding so badly only the day before, I scan the place. Thankfully, no one else is there. Yet.

"Pops, they didn't come back," I say, looking around like I can't believe our luck. "Is everything okay now?" I hold my breath for good news.

He looks at me, his once-bright blue irises having faded like a piece of newspaper too long in the sun. He was quite the looker in his younger days, but when life has given you more than your share of unkindnesses, this is one of the places it shows. These days, when I'm running around all the time, busy with my course and chasing after my younger sister, I don't often take the time to look—really look —at my father's face. And now that I do, I see a roadmap of all the crap that's come his way. His eyes are heavy-lidded, his brows grey, bushy, and wild, and it looks like he shaved that morning in the dark. There are some smooth spots on his face and some with uneven stubble. His complexion is a sort of grey-yellow, what I would expect of someone sick in the hospital.

A sadness grips my heart and I feel for the man. He's not been much of a father, but he sure has had his share of life's crappy handouts.

In answer to my question about visitors, he says nothing, only looks down at his feet, unintentionally bringing attention to his Hush Puppies, which are in desperate need of replacing.

That's the first thing I'll do when I get a job. A real job. I will buy my dad new shoes.

When it finally dawns on me that Pops isn't answering because he has only bad news to share, all the mountainous hope I have, that he can get himself out of the mess he's in, melts into a puddle of nothingness.

And manifests itself as a knot in my stomach so tight it takes my breath away, as the three Alekseev brothers appear from the back of the shop like some sort of nightmarish apparition. Only this is no dream. Without thinking, I position myself between my father and them. I know I can't stop them doing anything, but maybe I can be an obstacle, however temporary. Give my father time to get away.

Who am I kidding? Charleigh, the badass.

Not.

Instead of going after Pops like I'm sure they're going to, I find my feet leaving the floor as I am hoisted over someone's shoulder.

"Vadik, no," my father hollers.

"Oh my god," I scream, but it's hard to push out much air when all your weight is on your diaphragm, supported only by some beast's brawny shoulder.

So, I kick my legs around and pound on the man's back. If I can squirm enough to throw him off balance, he may drop me, giving me the chance to fight back.

Once again, who the hell am I kidding?

From my upside-down position, I don't see the guy with the shaved head, Vadik, but do see the two others. He must be the one carrying me. We head toward the back of the shop.

"Mr. Gates, stay right where you are. Niko will wait with you."

Oh god. What are they going to do? My mind races to the worst-case scenario, something all women fear with a devastating intensity, and I kick and scream harder. Vadik stops and waits for his brother, the one with the bun in his hair, to take a seat on a folding chair, and hands me to him like a sack of potatoes, like he does things like this all the time.

"You got her, Kir?"

I am laid across his lap like a bad girl about to get a spanking.

Holy shit.

I am about to get a spanking.

CHAPTER ELEVEN

Charleigh

Whack.

The first strike knocks the wind out of me.

Whack.

The second causes a muffled yell.

Whack.

And all those that follow leave me screaming for mercy.

Thank God I'm wearing blue jeans, which undoubtedly absorb some of the strikes.

After ten or so smacks—I lose count pretty quickly—Kir places his open palm on my bottom and rubs it in soft circles. The sting from the spanking is still there, but changes somehow. It hurts.

But also feels good.

"Do you think you can behave now? Not inter-fere in business that's not your own?" he asks.

I don't say anything, afraid of giving away the strange pleasure I'm experiencing.

In the absence of an answer, he fists my hair, wrenching my face to his. I claw at his painful grip but my efforts are useless. The only thing that works is when I finally answer his question.

"Y… yes," I sputter.

"Yes *what*?" he growls.

"Yes, I will behave now."

He sighs and Vadik takes me by the underarms, hoisting me to my feet. I am lightheaded from my head hanging down, and for a moment, I hold onto him until I'm steady.

Good god, he's solid. Unmovable. Like holding on to a mountain. And when I lift my head to look at him, his blue eyes sparkle like he's an actual human being. Which I know he is not.

We return to the front of the store, where Niko watches my father, now slumped in a chair, I'm pretty sure with tears dripping from his face.

Pops does not look at me.

"The contract is on the counter there," Kir says, gesturing to the glass case where pawned jewelry is kept as a weak attempt at security.

Pops tried to give my mother a piece once, a gold

bracelet someone had pawned, but she refused it. She didn't want anything that had come from some sort of distressed situation. When she put it that way, I felt the same. Too much bad juju. After that, I never tried on any of the jewelry again.

But he did once give her something he bought new. At least he said he did. And I have it now. Not that he knows. Or has ever noticed.

"Um, contract?" I ask with an involuntary squeak.

I look at the brothers, and then my father. No one responds.

"You're coming to work for us, Charleigh. Your father has signed the contract. This will all but erase his debt. Now you need to sign."

I scowl even as my behind stings from my spanking, a rush of fearlessness surging through me. "I'm not signing anything."

Kir looks at me like he wants to hit me. Like no one ever challenges him. Or if they do, they don't live to talk about it.

I want to drag my fingernails down his handsome face, leaving raw streaks of ripped flesh. Something that would hurt like hell, but what appeals most is how it would hurt his pride.

That, I would enjoy.

"I wouldn't sound so cavalier if I were you, Charleigh," Vadik says. "Your father has offered you."

That's a lie.

I look at Pops, who alarms me by doing everything he can to avoid my gaze. "No. No, Pops. You didn't."

He continues to look down, balled up in shame, and nods his head the tiniest bit. Just enough to let me know that yes, my very own father has sold me out.

How… how could he do this? In what world does this happen? And to *me*? I'm on the brink of a new life. I don't have time to work for these guys, whatever it is they want me to do.

My own father. I might not expect much of him, but *this*?

I clasp my stomach like someone punched me in the gut. I want to double over and sob, then beg, beg to be left alone.

The three brothers, handsome as they are, watch me coolly. There's no compassion in their eyes, nor pity. Just apathy. And indifference so ugly it almost takes their good looks down a notch.

Almost.

"What… what the hell can *I* offer *you*?" I ask, trying to steady my voice as I look from one man to the other.

"Sign here," Kir repeats.

I pick up the pen thrust in my direction. I've

never seen such a grave, determined expression on someone's face. And yet, I need to push one more time to try and help myself.

"What if I don't?" I say, mustering all the haughtiness I can.

Kir glances at Pops, then his brothers. Then me. "Well, we understand you have another sister. She might be kind of young but…"

Evie?

My stomach, already in bad shape, lurches and I can taste the bile that doesn't want to stay down. No, not Evie. Never Evie.

I'll die first.

"Fuck you," I spit at them.

Kir releases a booming laugh. "Those are big, dirty words for a virgin."

What did he just say?

He slowly approaches me, running his fingers through my tangled hair. I jerk away, and so he grabs a fistful, like it belongs to him.

Does it?

"Not only can we take your sister, Charleigh, but we will probably have to shoot your father, too. Right between the eyes."

This time, my legs buckle, but I am kept from reaching the floor due to Kir's grip on my hair. The pain is excruciating, and my vision is littered with funny dots of different colors and sizes, and I wonder if this is what it's like right before a person passes out.

"Up," he roars, pulling me by the hair.

A sob escapes. Then another. I lose my shit like I never have before, and ugly cry in front of all of them, and I don't care. I wail as my face distorts and I have snot running from my nose. I am breathing so hard I choke and cough, and no one does anything to help me catch my breath. The worst of it, though, is the pain in my chest where my heart is breaking. I clutch myself there, like I might split in two.

No one helps me.

No one is coming to help me.

CHAPTER TWELVE

In the farthest corner of the limo that I can, I bury my face in the expensive leather seat. The driver guns it, picking up speed, and I know we are on the freeway without even looking. I don't care where we are going. It doesn't matter. All that does, is that I'm being taken away.

I curl myself into a ball, a shell that will keep these men away from me. And yet, in the confines of the limo, their words easily reach my ears, no matter how much I want to drown them out.

"With a little work, she'll do quite nicely."

"Small tits, but what can you do?"

"Hey they're better than those giant things so many of the girls have these days."

I want to crawl away in shame at their offensive evaluation.

Actually, I want to die.

I don't know what lies ahead, but I do know it can't be good. And the fact that my father has completely and totally sold me out is a pain I'm not sure I can live with. My heart hurts. It literally hurts.

Even worse than when my mother died.

We pull up to what must be the guys' place of business, an old warehouse-looking building with blacked-out windows, and they direct me to a door, also painted a dull black with no exterior handle. If I didn't know better, I'd think this was another abandoned building in a bad part of town. But when the door opens from the inside as if someone's watching for us, a statuesque woman ushers us in. For a moment, I wonder if she'll help me. Another woman will surely understand my plight, won't she? So, with Kir's death grip still on my arm, I head straight for her, getting as close as I can. But when I see her eyes in the dim light, really see them, I realize I am well and truly fucked.

CHAPTER THIRTEEN

"This is *her*? The one you told me about?"

Dominika looks Charleigh up and down with clear displeasure. I'm not sure whether she truly disapproves or is just flexing her muscle. Until my Uncle Mikey fled the country a few weeks back, my brothers and I were only peripherally involved with the club. So, perhaps understandably, she's resentful we've taken over. She feels pushed aside. Irritated by our new hands-on approach. But if she doesn't watch her shitty attitude, she'll really be pushed aside—like *out on the street* pushed aside.

It's no secret why my father kept her around all these years. Uncle Mikey did the same, but for different reasons, primarily so he didn't have to do a minute of work, that is, aside from draining the club's accounts. The woman had free rein of the place for the better part of Mikey's reign. She's used to being the queen bee.

But those days are over, and if she can't hack it, she knows where the goddamn door is.

"Her name is Charleigh, Dominika. Charleigh Gates. To pay her father's debts, she's working for us now."

Dominika sneers distastefully at Charleigh's blue jeans and well-worn sneakers. I have no doubt the girl's lack of makeup and simple braid are driving her crazy too.

She often laments how American women dress like men. So casual, without a care for who they might see on the street, she says.

For all the years I've known her, seeing her at Papa's club as well as at family social gatherings, she's always had her overly-dyed red hair teased several inches above the crown of her head, and worn enough makeup for two, maybe even three women. While she's statuesque, the result is not attractive, and is even less so as she's not aged well due to her smoking and other unhealthy habits. In fact, when we were kids, I mean really little, my brothers and I thought for a time she was a witch.

We still laugh when we talk about that.

"Wh… what is this place?" Charleigh asks, her eyes wide.

Yeah, she's scared. She should be. I mean, her bastard father sold her out and she has no idea what's coming next. It's too bad. She seems like a nice kid. But life isn't fair and anyone who says otherwise is a fucking idiot.

"We do a variety of things here, Charleigh. We have card games, exotic dancers, a lounge, and even provide our members more *intimate* adult entertainment when it's called for." Even though Charleigh is quite tall, Dominika, in her six-inch heels, manages to look down on her, establishing dominance like a wolf in the wild.

This is not lost on Charleigh, who looks around nervously. "Do you… do you mean strippers? Well, I… I can't dance."

Dominika laughs like the haughty bitch that she is. "Don't worry, darling. We'll have you serve drinks. That's where everyone starts."

"And the intimate entertainment? Or whatever you called it. Isn't that illegal?"

"What isn't?" Dominika mocks, revealing her crooked yellow teeth. No wonder my brothers and I were afraid of her as kids. "Welcome to our world."

She knows exactly what we plan to use Charleigh

for. And she's smart enough not to let that cat out of the bag. Yet.

On one hand, I understand Dominika's scrutiny of Charleigh. At first glance she doesn't look like much. Lanky, small tits, skin so white she's almost a ghost. But when you look a moment longer and a little deeper, you can't miss her blue eyes like a pool so deep you could get lost in them, nor her full lips, which will be captivating with a little red smeared on them. Her hair is long and lustrous and a hairdresser will be able to work wonders with it.

In short, the woman is an enchanting blank slate. That's the best we can hope for in our line of work. Like a holy grail. Its value is nearly impossible to estimate.

But what is perhaps most treasured of all is her alleged virginity. We will, of course, have a doctor verify the fact, but her loser father swore she's never had a boyfriend when he was trying to sell us on her.

He better not be lying. At the same time, I don't know how a man can talk about his daughter in those terms. I guess that's what you do when you're a desperate motherfucker. He might have reduced his immediate problems by shoving her off on us, but I can guarantee that once the dust settles, he'll hate himself for the rest of his days for what he did.

Not my problem, though.

If Gates was telling the truth about his daughter, and I really mean *if*, she'll fetch a pretty penny at auction. Although, I have my doubts. What twenty-year-old American girl has not been fucked by some idiot? But if his claim is true, this will set the club on track for massive success, wiping out the financial woes caused by Uncle Mikey, and even providing the cash needed to expand our operations, should we decide to. We can stop babysitting the club and get back to our more profitable ventures.

Papa would be proud.

While Charleigh's clearly scared, it's not keeping her from shooting questions our way. Her voice gets more high-pitched the more we deny her answers. This is standard operating procedure. It keeps the new girls off-balance. Increases their discomfort. And in the end, helps assure their compliance. Compliance is good in our business. Keeps the drama to a minimum.

"Where are we going now?" she asks.

Dominika is already bored with her, so Niko and I take her to her new accommodations.

Accessible only by elevator, the top floor of the club was long ago converted to suites that rented by special, privileged members, often by the hour. Since my brothers and I took over, we've started staying in them so we can keep any eye on everything going on. The staff are getting used to seeing us around twenty-four-seven, a shock since Uncle Mikey only ever swung by to raid the cash drawer.

Fucker.

I lock Charleigh in her room, which is probably nicer than anything she's ever seen in her life, and I head to my own to kick back for a bit. Vadik and Niko are watching sports together, so I can finally have a little time to myself.

That is, until it dawns on me that my room shares a wall with Charleigh's and I can clearly hear her crying.

CHAPTER FOURTEEN

For fuck's sake.

All I want to do is relax. This week has been one pain in the ass after another, from cash going 'missing' from one of our liquor stores to someone pulling a gun at one of our card games. Instead of chilling out, I have to listen to this woman lose her shit. So, I put on my noise-cancelling headphones and turn on some music I haven't listened to in a while.

A lilting, French café song fills my ears, and I lean back in my chair and close my eyes, transported to happier days. Before I knew what searing pain and longing were.

Before my beloved was killed.

I adjust the volume of her recorded music. It's

really the only thing I have left of her. When she was killed, her asshole parents swept in and removed every trace of her from our home.

I was too grief-stricken at the time to stop them, catatonic as I was for the better part of a year.

I take a deep breath as she finishes a song that's always been one of my favorites. I remember her singing it onstage with a flower behind her ear, her lips nearly kissing the mic, staring at me like I was the only person in the room.

We might have been in a crowded club, but it was always just the two of us.

I didn't deserve her. If she were alive, I'd tell her that.

My eyes fall closed and I am remembering her scent when a hand lands on my shoulder, startling the shit out of me. My eyes fly open. I yank the headphones off, and the room fills with Clara's lovely voice.

"Fuck, Niko, you scared the shit out me," I yell.

My brother takes a step back, hands up, as if in surrender. "Easy man. I knocked several times but no answer. When you have those headphones on, you can't hear a goddamn thing."

"Yeah. That's kind of the point."

Niko looks at the headphones, now on the floor

where I dropped them, Clara's lilting song pouring out of them.

I know what he's going to say. He's said it a hundred times before.

And he'll say it again.

"I don't know why you do this to yourself, man."

No, he doesn't know. He never will. No one will.

It's my cross to bear.

"What'd you come by for, Nik?" I ask.

He tilts his head toward the wall that my room shares with Charleigh's. "I guess you heard her, huh?"

I nod, grabbing my headphones off the floor and shutting down my phone's music app.

My brother Niko's a good guy. Almost too good. He can be a hard ass when he needs to, but he's also the kind of person who finds a spider in the house and goes out of his way to move it outside before someone stomps on it.

He's always been that way, unlike Vadik and me. And there's a reason for that, if you ask me.

"I was thinking of going to talk to her," he starts to say.

Oh, Christ.

"You can't do that, Niko. You know you can't. And what would you say, anyway? We're selling your virgin ass for beaucoup bucks to some rich mother-fucker? I bet she'd love to hear that."

"I feel for her, Kir—" he starts to say.

I stop him. "I know you do, man, but you know the rules. You know how we do things. Same as we always have. That's not gonna change."

He's a kind-hearted man, Niko is. Much more so than Vadik and me. And he knows what betrayal feels like. So, he's got something in common with this chick. Thus, the empathy.

Although he has empathy for everyone.

Which means we need to watch him at all times.

Not five minutes later, we're summoned to dinner. We settle into the opulent dining room and are served the incredible food Chef always prepares for us.

"Chef, can you make sure the woman in the guest room also gets a nice plate of this for herself?" Niko asks.

"Of course, Mr. Alekseev," he says, heading back to the kitchen.

Goddamn if Chef isn't one talented mother-fucker. I dig into my filet mignon and the tender meat melts in my mouth.

But Vadik hasn't picked up his utensils yet.

In between bites—I'm fucking starving—I glance at him and find he's looking at Niko.

Actually, he's not just looking at him. He's glaring at him.

And this eventually dawns on Niko, too. He looks at our brother, frowning. "What? What's up your ass?"

Vadik rolls his head back on his neck like he's trying to shake out some tension and returns his gaze to our brother. "Why did you ask for a plate of food for Charleigh? We weren't going to let her starve for Christ's sake."

Niko shrugs. "Guess I wanted her to have a plate of the good stuff."

"Nik, you gotta keep your pecker in your pants. Don't be getting any ideas about that girl. She's our cash cow, and we're gonna exploit that like the motherfuckers we are. Don't be going sweet on her."

Vadik knows wanting something too much, especially a woman, is a sure recipe for trouble. We all know that. And Niko doesn't appreciate being reminded.

He grinds his teeth. He might be the soft one of the three of us, but that doesn't mean he doesn't get pissed at his big brother. "She was crying, asshole. I could hear it. Kir heard it too. So, I thought a nice dinner was in order. That's all. Calm the fuck down. I saw you looking at her too, my friend."

Niko might have pushed back, but it's obvious

Vadik's message is loud and clear. He picks up his fork and knife and dives into his dinner.

"Chef!" he hollers a minute later.

"Yes, Mr. Alekseev?" he asks, his head poking out from the kitchen.

"Get Dominika up here. We need to talk to her." He adds *please* as an afterthought.

Typical Vadik.

Chef nods. "Shall I prepare a place for her at the table?"

My brother shakes his head with force. "No. Absolutely not."

That Dominika will see this as a huge slight, not being invited to join our meal, is not lost on Vadik. In some ways, the two of them are similar, with their desire to be 'head bitch in charge,' as Niko calls it. We do have some pressing things to discuss with her, but I, personally, would not have invited her to a meeting that includes watching us eat a fabulous dinner.

But Vadik Is a douche that way.

CHAPTER FIFTEEN

KIR

"Gentlemen," Dominika says in greeting about ten minutes later. She looks around the table and when she sees there is no place set for her, instantly gets the message. Almost imperceptibly, because she's good like that, her head jerks in response. She knows she's being dissed. And bless her, she forces herself into a semi-smiling façade of pleasantness.

It must be excruciating.

"What can I do for you?" she asks from across the room where she remains standing. Like a servant.

Vadik takes a bite of his steak, followed up by a swig of wine, just to make her wait. Classic Vadik, making her cool her heels.

And if I didn't have the level of self-preservation I do, I'd laugh out loud at their juvenile tug-of-war.

"Domi, how are you preparing for the auction? Can you pull it together in time?" he asks, dabbing his face with a napkin.

She hates that nickname. Which is exactly why my brother uses it.

I steal a look at Niko, whose eyebrows are raised. Everyone watches their scuffle. No one says a thing.

"Yes, Vadik, I'm calling all the high rollers right now. I'm about halfway through the list. One may fly in from Saudi Arabia."

Jesus Christ. That means big money. Big fucking money. If men like that see something they want, they bid it up until no one else can afford it.

Because no one has more money than they do.

Bastards.

But if all goes according to plan, we'll have ourselves a chunk of their fucking money, and soon too.

"I passed by the girl's room a moment ago. Looks like she's having a nice dinner," Dominika says, looking around the table.

It's funny, how much one look can say. She's pissed. When my father was running the joint, he treated her like a queen. And when Uncle was in charge, he let her do whatever the fuck she wanted.

But now that my brothers and I are in charge? Shit's different.

Way different.

Niko, always the peacemaker, chimes in. "Yeah, she was having a hard time of it, so I thought a nice dinner would do her good."

Dominika couldn't give a shit.

Seriously. If the girl starved, the woman wouldn't bat an eye.

Vadik continues. "You'll be getting her ready this week, won't you?"

"Absolutely. She'll look like a million bucks by the time I'm done with her."

Dominika excels in this area. I've seen her turn many a girl off the street into women who resemble runway models.

It's like staging a home. The nicer it looks, the more it sells for. Common sense, really.

Vadik nods, his mood visibly improved. His commitment to the club borders on obsessive, just like being the oldest perfect son does. "Good. Good work. There's a bonus in this for you, Dominika, if all goes according to plan. The girl has great potential."

At this, her face brightens. "I agree, boss. She'll fetch a pretty penny."

She heads for the door, any insults forgotten. When there is money involved, Dominika is nothing if not predictable.

It looks like our lovely Charleigh will not be in house for very long. Which is probably just as well. I can already see Niko has it over for her, and I'd be lying if I didn't admit I want to get to know her better myself. Not necessarily deflower her, but I'd relish teaching her the ways of a sensuous woman.

I'd be patient the first time she took my dick into her mouth, telling her to taste my precum before she lets my length run over her tongue. I'd tickle her throat to help her relax so she can take me as deeply as a woman is supposed to do shit like that.

After a minute, I'd hold her head as I pumped her face, but not too hard. Don't want to scare her off, at least the first time. Let the hard shit come later, with some other guy.

Open your throat for me, my beauty, I'd say.

Just like how I trained Clara. She'd suck my dick anytime of the day or night. She was amazing.

And for fuck's sake, I can't deny it any longer. Charleigh looks like her. Not identical, but close enough to cause any of us a double-take. Vadik and Niko have noticed. And they are watching me.

As is Dominika.

And you know what?

They can all fuck right off.

CHAPTER SIXTEEN

Charleigh

"Wake up. Wake up, dammit."

I gasp, making the violent transition from slumberland to my cruel new reality. Even if someone weren't violently shaking me by the shoulder, and I'd woken up on my own, it would still have taken only seconds to remember the hellhole my life has fallen into.

If you're lucky, dreams take you away from your waking problems. When I lost my mother, nighttime was the only break I got in an otherwise twenty-four-hour cycle of horrific grief. In the 'beforetimes' I'd wake up in my simple but sunny bedroom with thoughts of the day ahead. Who would I walk to school with? Had I finished my homework? What would I have for lunch? Then, I'd abruptly remember none of that stuff mattered anymore. Not a bit of it. Mother was gone. I'd never see her again. My view of the world switched from color to a dull black and white in one wretched moment.

But with Dominika peering down on me in my bed, there's no momentary forgetting the turn my life has taken. There's no transition, sudden or otherwise, from the innocence of dreamland to wakefulness. It's probably just as well. Why postpone the inevitable? Why go through the agony of realizing nothing is as it seemed only seconds before?

With the covers yanked down to my ankles, I shiver in the freezing room. I wasn't provided anything to sleep in, so I just wore my panties to bed. Fortunately, my bed does have a nice, fluffy down comforter—strangely luxurious for someone who's essentially a prisoner. I get to my feet before Dominika touches me again, my arms flying to cover my chest. I stand before her, pale, shivering, covered in goosebumps.

She looks around the room. "Why isn't there any heat in this goddamned place?" she snaps.

Locating a thermostat, she marches over to it like she's mad at it. She punches a few buttons and nods in approval. A whoosh fills the room, and a baseboard heater begins to blow warm air.

At least they're giving me heat.

Actually, the room I am sequestered in is unexpectedly nice. Being kidnapped-slash-sold off by my father didn't leave me much hope of ending up anyplace other than a dump. The room the guys dropped me in has a large and comfortable mattress, I'm happy to find, and the softest sheets I've ever touched. The bed itself is a feminine all-white four-poster, with a matching dresser on one wall and a beautiful vanity on the other. And even though I know we are in an undesirable part of town, being on the top floor provides a view that stretches for miles.

The contradiction is almost too much to grasp.

Like, *really*?

I didn't absorb any of this, where I was or what I was surrounded by the night before when I arrived. Hysteria will do that to a person. All I could focus on was how life as I knew it was over, and what lay ahead looked to be pretty freaking dreadful.

"Put your arms down," Dominika barks. "Now turn around," she demands, twirling her finger for emphasis.

I slowly rotate, I presume so she can check me out, maybe to do some sort of assessment. I am hoping against hope that she finds some sort of deficiency—crooked teeth, a strange BO smell, even an ingrown toenail—and report back to the guys that I can't possibly add any value to their operation there at the club. That I am ugly, skinny, flat-chested, and generally useless, and that they made a mistake bringing me here. And that they should return me to my father without delay.

If only I were so lucky.

But hope, faith, optimism—whatever you want to call it—doesn't give a damn. Not about me, or anybody. At ten years old, when I yearned for my mother to be returned to me, she wasn't. My pleas didn't fall on deaf ears. They fell on *no* ears. There's no fairy godmother looking out for us—at least not for me. And I know full well no matter how much I wish it, I'm not about to be sent home from this place for my inadequacies. Dominika looks like the resourceful type. She will force-mold me into whatever she and the guys want, deficiencies be damned.

Clicking her tongue, she shakes her head with disapproval. "What are the guys thinking with this one?" she mutters under her breath, not so much to avoid offending me—I doubt that would even cross her mind—but because she's just thinking out loud.

"Let me see your teeth again," she barks.

I open my mouth like a horse at auction, careful not to breathe on her since I haven't brushed my teeth yet.

She seems not to notice.

Then she steps even closer and pulls down the skin below my right eye, then moves on to my left. Her gaze travels to my shoulders and arms, my breasts, and to my stomach. She swats my tummy so fast I don't have time to flinch, again mumbling under her breath. "Solid. At least there's that."

Chalk one up for me!

"You're flat as hell, but some men like that. They're getting tired of the giant fake tits so many girls have." She nods approvingly, or at least as approvingly as she's inclined. "Now, pull down your underpants."

Really? What the hell does she need me to do that for?

But before I can find out, and because I hesitated with my thumbs hooked in the elastic of my bikini panties, she grabs them herself and rips them to my ankles. I am now stark naked. And this time I don't cover anything up. Why bother?

"Ugh. Do you really have the full bush thing going on there? Don't you know all the girls your age are waxing or shaving that thing these days?"

She looks at me. She really expects an answer.

So I shrug, not sure what I can say that will satisfy her. "Um. Well, no. I don't make a habit of asking my friends about their pubic hair."

Her eyes narrow at my minor sarcasm, and she

shakes her head like I'm hopeless. "We'll get you cleaned up down there before your physical."

Physical? Cleaned-up? Huh?

I don't ask. I don't need to. She sees the confusion written all over my face.

She rolls her eyes impatiently. Like I should know all this. As if being nabbed by my father's debt holders is an everyday thing. "You'll be examined by a doctor. Blood tests, hymen test, all that business."

CHAPTER SEVENTEEN

CHARLEIGH

Hymen test? What in God's name is that?

"Wh… why?" I ask, wrapping my arms around myself again, creating a little shell of protection.

She huffs loudly. "First, to make sure you don't have any STDs. Or at least any that aren't curable." She drops her head back and cackles like a witch. "And then, to make sure you really are a virgin."

"I… I don't understand," I sputter.

"Honey, you may start out serving drinks, but that's not all you're going to do here. If you're really a virgin, like your creep father said you are, you're going to be making the Alekseev brothers a lot of money."

The disgusting taste of bile rises in my mouth

and I try hard to swallow it away. I was brought a nice dinner the night before but managed to choke down only a few bites. I'm now so hungry I'm light headed, and Dominika's casual comments about my future compound my nausea.

"I… I think I'm going to be sick," I whisper, bringing my hand to my mouth.

Taking me by the upper arm, Dominika shoves me to a seat on the edge of the bed. "Here," she says with a push, "put your head between your knees. It'll pass. Take some deep breaths."

I close my eyes and wish I were anywhere else. Really, anywhere. I don't care where. Just someplace that's not the Alekseev brothers' club. Or whatever the hell this weird place is.

When the fainting sensation passes, that's the only thing that's improved. I look up at Dominika. "What do you mean about being a virgin? And making money?"

She puts her hands on her hips. "Look. Don't worry about that for now. Just throw on this robe. We're going to the salon."

I catch the plushy robe she throws in my direction but am stung by new fear. "Don't I need to put on something more than this? If we're going out to a salon?"

She gestures for me to get a move on. "We're not leaving the premises. We have a salon here."

Here? At this nasty place? This creepy warehouse hiding a fancy bedroom and sumptuous dinners also has a *salon?*

It's so… disorienting. Even if they don't have big plans for me, the jumbling in my brain is enough torture.

I pull on the thick robe, nothing like the tattered one I have at home, and follow Dominika out of my room. As my bare feet slap the floor beneath me, nearly drowned out by the sky-high platform shoes Dominika is wearing, I take in my surroundings in a way I wasn't able to before, hysterical as I was.

The hallway is dark, not in a creepy way but in a fancy-chic style with glittery chandeliers and gold-painted trim around the doors. Up ahead I see one that's slightly open, so I slow my walk, pretending to adjust my robe, and glance inside as I pass. I catch a sliver of the brother with the dirty blond hair, Niko, and before I am out of sight, he glances up from his desk, a corner of his mouth upturned as he lays his eyes on me.

It's a momentary sighting, but as horrified as I am by my situation, I also get a strange rush that a man so exquisitely handsome smiles at me. And before we get much further down the hall, he calls after Dominika and me.

"Ladies, how are things?" he says from his door.

In the dim hallway light, he's better looking than the night before, if that's possible. He has a little unshaven scruff on his face, and his necktie is loosened. His belt hangs nicely around his hips, emphasizing an incredibly flat stomach. He walks toward us in two or three steps, that's how long his legs are.

And I am shaking so hard.

He might have been calling the two of us, but he doesn't even glance at Dominika. His gaze is locked on mine. I wish I'd thought to brush my hair or something before leaving my room because I'm a horrible mess. In the robe and along with my bare feet, I must look like some sad little orphan.

Before I can answer him, not that I know what to say anyway, Dominika is by my side, her chin raised and her lips tight around what looks to be an utterly fake smile. "Everything's coming along, Niko," she says. "Just taking the new girl to the salon to see if we can fix her up a bit."

She looks me up and down disdainfully, because she can. I so want to do the same back to her. The woman is *no* freaking prize. I mean, has she looked in the mirror, with that orange hair and caked-on makeup? She's repulsive.

Jesus.

Niko continues eyeing me and gets closer, acting like Dominika hasn't said a word. As if she's not even there. When he reaches us, he takes a hank of my hair, slowly twirling it in his fingers as if it's the most fascinating thing he's ever seen.

I consider pulling away from him, even though it won't do any good or change my circumstances. But I don't. While I have no power over my situation, I oddly want him to continue. In spite of the fact that I am essentially a prisoner, taken against my will—even if I did sign a damn contract—I am calmed by his touch. I want more.

But that's not happening, at least not right now.

Dominika grabs me by the upper arm and pulls me away from Niko's touch. He looks away from me only to scowl at her, but she's not deterred. Turning her back on him, she drags me down the hall without so much as a word.

And while she yanks me so hard I nearly lose my balance, I do manage to look back over my shoulder, where I find Niko watching me with that half smile. When our eyes meet, he gives me a slight nod, as if to say...

As if to say what?

That everything will be okay?

Yeah, right.

I have no doubt I am imagining his affection. That man cares nothing for my well-being. If he did, he wouldn't have brought me here and locked me up.

CHAPTER EIGHTEEN

CHARLEIGH

To call the room Dominika takes me to a 'salon' is being ridiculously generous. It's big enough for one padded treatment table and a bookcase filled with everything I suppose they need to 'fix me up.'

I've read about 'spa days' and 'spa treatments' in the fashion magazines I occasionally buy. They seem like something affluent women do all the time, often with their friends.

I can't imagine such an indulgence, being pampered from head to toe alongside your buddies, like you're a freaking goddess. I wonder if afterwards, these women float through life for days, feeling important and beautiful and spoiled.

Luci and I have talked about having a spa day someday, after we finish our courses and are working women with good jobs. It's not something we'd do all the time. Really, we just want to try it once. For a treat.

And here I am, having my first spa experience. Only not at a spa, not with my friend, and not to be pampered.

Dominika overwhelms the small room with her presence. "Give her a trim, fix those eyebrows, wax that pussy, and give her a mani-pedi," she barks at a small woman in a white coat.

"Will do, Miss Dominika," she says with an obedient nod.

"Hello," the woman says to me when Dominika pulls the door shut behind her. While we're in close quarters and need to keep shuffling out of each other's way, I can already breathe better. "Let's get the hard part out of the way." She slides the robe from my shoulders and hangs it on the door.

I'm not sure I'll ever get used to being naked in front of strangers.

"Lay on your back here on the table," she says after pulling some crinkly white paper down to protect it. "Pull your knees up and put the bottom of your feet together. Like a frog."

Gross.

I lay on the table and, in spite of the woman's

instructions, clamp my knees together tightly while she stirs something in a little electric pot.

When she faces me, she rolls her eyes. "Are you going to make this more difficult than it has to be? C'mon. Spread 'em."

I place the soles of my feet together, and let my knees drops to the sides of the table exposing myself in a way I never have for anyone other than my doctor.

Like a *frog*.

The woman grabs my feet and pushes them toward me, further spreading my legs, and I want to die from the embarrassment. But the worst is yet to come.

To my horror, with gloved hands, she roughly pulls apart my labia, spreading hot wax on one side with a stick. After a few seconds—maybe longer, I'm not sure—she removes it with a violent tug, taking with it one half of my pubic hair and I'm sure several layers of skin. I scream from a pain so intense a wave of nausea passes over me, and before I know it, she does the other side, then pushes my knees to my chest so she can get to my ass.

How will I be able to sit?

"Stop breathing like that," she scolds. "You'll hyperventilate."

She puts a cool compress on my screaming crotch and lifts my head to help me take a sip of water. I want to cry over what seems like a little act of kindness, her small effort to comfort me, but the truth is the woman is just doing her job. She doesn't give a crap about me.

This initial torture is followed by a couple hours of trimming, tweezing, filing, and painting, a breeze after my rough start. As if on cue, Dominika shows up and looks at me with some semblance of satisfaction. "Better. This is better."

I don't know whether to laugh or cry. I ask for another ice pack for my crotch.

The spa lady gets one while Dominika tosses my robe at me. I follow her to a dressing room with racks of what look like very skimpy clothing, and a long table lined with chairs and makeup mirrors.

"This is Stacey. She'll get you ready for your shift."

And she leaves me with a small, pretty woman whose hair is pulled back so she can put on her makeup.

In between applying her false eyelashes, Stacey looks at me sympathetically. I want to fall into her arms. She has no idea what it means to come across someone nice in this place.

Or maybe she does.

CHAPTER NINETEEN

CHARLEIGH

"Hey," she says. "I'll show you how to do your makeup and then help you choose an outfit."

It's all I can do not to cry. Stacey is patient and tries to make small talk, but I can only manage one-word answers. She seems to understand, and while I want to ask her if she's in the same situation I am, I know if I start talking about it, I'll lose my shit. I relinquish the ice pack and she helps me into stockings, a short skirt, bustier, and the highest heels I've ever worn. I look ridiculous. Like a Halloween costume store's idea of a streetwalker.

She pats my arms. "Don't worry, you don't have to walk far in those things. All you have to do is take orders and bring the men their drinks. It's pretty easy. Sometimes you even get tips, although we're not supposed to accept them." She lowers her voice. "But we all do."

"Wait, I'm starting now? Serving drinks? It's not even noon yet."

She shrugs. "I know. But the club is open twenty-four hours. Members come anytime they want."

Looking me up and down with approval, she leads me to a lounge where the light is dim and music is playing low. There is a murmur of male voices, nothing loud, just quiet chatting and occasional laughter, and leaves me there. The bartender waves me over.

"So you're the new girl. Here's your tray. You'd better take this notepad and pen until you've been at this awhile."

I stare at him, unable to move.

He sighs deeply. "See that table on the other side of the room? The one with the three men?"

I nod.

"Okay. They just got here. Go ask them what they want to drink. It's that easy."

I gulp, pulling on my short skirt as if that will afford me a little modesty, and cross the room.

"Looks like someone new today," an older man with grandfatherly silver hair says, looking me up and down.

I have a feeling I'm going to get used to being gawked at. It will be nice when I don't even notice it anymore. If that day ever comes.

"May… may I bring you something to drink?" I ask in a trembling voice.

The younger man at the table, with a long beard, guffaws. "There's nothin' to be afraid of, honey. We won't bite. Will we, boys?" he asks, looking at his friends.

"I can't say we won't bite. But I can say we won't bite too *hard,*" the third one says, and they break into peals of laughter.

I force a smile and even a bit of laughter to ease my tension. They give me their order and I return with three bourbons a couple minutes later.

As I set the last one down, somebody's hand finds my ass. I jump, nearly spilling the drink, and quickly back out of reach of the man with the beard.

I open my mouth to scold him, but something stops me. This place isn't the real world, so real world rules don't apply here. I can't slap a man for touching me the way I can on the outside. I can't throw a drink in his face, nor can I scream at him.

What am I supposed to do?

I slink away to the next table, and then the next, and before I know it, I am running drinks back and forth like a delivery robot. But the last straw is when some guy smacks my ass so hard, the drinks I'm carrying go flying off the tray.

I watch them tumble to the floor, ice cubes bouncing in all directions, the alcohol disappearing into the carpet.

I run back to the dressing room where I double over in tears.

Not a minute later, Dominika finds me. "What the hell is going on here?"

"I... I..." I sputter. But I can't get the words out.

Until a sharp smack across my face forces a scream. I'm so stunned, rubbing my burning cheek, that I stop crying and look into Dominika's dark, dispassionate eyes.

"Get it together, young lady. Or things will get worse for you."

Worse? How could things get any worse?

"This is your new reality, and you need to accept it. Grow the fuck up. Your life on easy street is over now, little fool. You're not above any of this and quit bellyaching like you are." She steps closer to me and points a finger inches from my face. "If there's one thing I can't stand, it's a prissy little bitch. Get it together, Charleigh. So help me."

Her eyes narrow and her lips press into a thin, ugly line, emphasizing her sloppy lip liner. I want to tell her that her lousy makeup job adds about ten years to her appearance, but I would also like to live to see tomorrow.

I blow my nose and get back to work.

What the hell else can I do?

CHAPTER TWENTY

Niko

Unbeknownst to my brothers, I spent the better part of the morning watching, via our closed-circuit camera feed, the cocktail lounge where Charleigh works. The woman is a beauty by any measure, but with her hair and makeup done, she could rival a movie star. Her cocktail waitress outfit, designed to turn the guests on and get them thinking of ways they might like to spend their big bucks with us, is cute as hell on her, though I'm sure she hates it.

But that's okay.

She'll get used to it.

On her first shift, she was a little wobbly in her heels, but after a few days in the lounge, she's pretty steady now, and if I'm not mistaken, has even started to shake her ass a bit when she walks. The lacy tops of her thigh-highs are just visible under her short, swingy skirt, and her bustier gives her just enough cleavage to tempt any man.

Especially me.

I don't meet many girl-next-door types, which Charleigh personifies flawlessly. Seeing her transformation has been like watching a caterpillar turn into a butterfly.

Not that there is anything wrong with the caterpillar.

There's a reason why every guy fantasizes about the girl next door. She's usually the first girl any boy knows, aside from sisters and cousins. And even though our tastes may change as we get older, we nearly all still have a thing for the unassuming, natural cutie who was once the object of our frequent fantasies. Hell, I jerked off so much at that age I was sure my dick would fall off. At least that's what they told us at the Catholic school we attended until Vadik's fighting got us kicked out.

So yeah, I might have a little boyhood crush on our new girl Charleigh. But I have it under control. It won't impact the way we do anything around here. Besides, I'm not alone. Vadik looks at her as if he's about to drop to one knee and freaking propose, and Kir can't take his eyes off her because she resembles Clara, the woman he lost.

As it turns out, we three are not alone in finding Charleigh attractive. A couple of the old pervs who frequent the club haven't been able to keep their hands to themselves during her shifts. That's to be expected, and is usually tolerated. Like we always say, we want to get the bastards thinking with their little heads. That's when they start spending real money. Their grab-ass antics are usually pretty harmless. The only time I've ever had to step in and get involved was with a particularly handsy guest who had way too much to drink. Turned out he was going through a bad divorce, and the waitress reminded him of his soon-to-be ex. He pushed her to the ground and straddled her, ready to throw a closed-fist punch until the bartender tackled him.

Needless to say, the man was never permitted back here. He'll never throw a punch again, and in fact, he won't write, shave, hold a fork, or wipe his ass with his right hand, either.

That's how serious we are about the few rules we have. And punching out a waitress is against the fucking rules.

When Charleigh finishes today's three-hour shift, I decide to stretch my legs and say hello. But before I do, I turn to the camera in the hallway just outside the lounge and see her stop on her way out. I turn on the sound.

It takes me seconds to realize she's speaking with Dimitri Yegorov, and from the look of it, he's traveling with his usual posse of flatterers.

"Ah, here is a new girl. I do not know you," his voice croons through the tinny sound system. He lifts Charleigh's hand and brings it to his lips.

"What is your name, beautiful?" he asks, still holding her hand.

She sniffles. If Dominika sees that, she'll be all over her. She hates girls who cry. "Um, my name is Charleigh."

Dimitri laughs. "Interesting name for a woman. But Americans do things different from us Russians, right, boys?"

His hangers-on nod and express their agreement with him like he said something brilliant.

I doubt they ever do otherwise. They wouldn't dare. He's bad news.

And we don't like him.

In fact, we prefer he stay as far away from our club as possible, but the *Pakhan* feels it's better for the region if we permit him and his friends. So, Dimitri shows up here as often as possible, not only because our club is one-of-a-kind, but also to rub our faces in the fact that he can come and go as he pleases.

As inconceivable as it is, we have a lifelong

connection to this guy. We played together as children and our families spent holidays and vacations together. Our fathers founded this club, my Papa and his. One might think that since our fathers are now gone, we'd take up where they left off and be the best of business partners. But no. Not by a longshot.

Dimitri's dad, when he passed, left my dad as sole owner. The club became one hundred percent his, and now that Papa's gone, it belongs to my brothers and me. Dimitri has his own opinions about how and why this happened, but the facts are incontestable. Mr. Yegorov left the club to my dad. Not his son. It's that simple, and Dimitri has been angry about it for years. He feels he still owns an interest in it because it was, in his mind, somehow wrested away from his papa.

Which is part of the reason my brothers and I suspect he's behind the house fire that killed our parents.

CHAPTER TWENTY-ONE

When I think about it, and how Dimitri has the nerve to show his ugly face as often as he does around here, my fingers itch to wrap themselves around his neck.

And squeeze.

So, I don't think about it too much. Unless it's being rubbed in my face, like right now.

I blow up the video on my monitor so I can see exactly what he's up to, holding Charleigh's hand and pulling her closer. I don't like it. I don't like that he's touching her. I don't like that he is even looking at her.

"My poor girl," he croons like he's some sort of gentleman. "Why are you sad? Are they not treating you well here?" He looks around at his buddies, who nod like the toadies they are.

"I… I am adjusting. I'll be fine, really," Charleigh insists, attempting to back away from him.

The girl has good instincts, I'll give her that.

"Where do you come from, child?" he asks, as if he's really interested.

He hands her his handkerchief and she blows her nose, oblivious to how he's eating her up with his eyes.

While she explains she's local and talks about her dad's shop, the whole time Dimitri is licking his chops, most likely trying to figure out when he can get into her pants. If there's anyone with a fetish for new blood, it's him.

But he will never get his hands on Charleigh.

That's when I stop watching the camera feed and hustle down the hall to interrupt their little rendezvous.

"Dimitri!" I say as if I'm happy to see him.

Fucker knows I hate him. But inside the club, I pretend otherwise. At least, I try to.

I clap him on the back, a little harder than I would anybody else. Just to be a dick, of course, and as I do, he inches closer to the oblivious Charleigh, who is trying her hardest to smile in a situation she doesn't know how to handle.

"Niko, my friend," Dimitri booms. His minions follow his lead, smiling broadly with their hands clasped in front of them.

I don't know how he can stand being followed around by a bunch of suck-ups. But right now, I want him the fuck away from Charleigh.

I shake his extended hand because, what choice do I have, making a mental note to run to the men's room as soon as I'm free to scrub off his slime.

As if on cue, Dimitri throws an arm around Charleigh's shoulders to see how I react. I know exactly what he's doing, and he knows I know, and yet we must still have this fucking standoff.

It's like a fight you get into as a kid. Circling, sizing each other up, waiting for someone to throw the first punch. Except that as adults, we don't throw actual punches. We do shit like use veiled threats and draw firearms.

Some things don't change. Much.

Charleigh looks at me, her eyes wide. I have no doubt she picked up on the tension between Dimitri and me. And now she's looking to me for answers. What to do next. What is expected of her?

I don't blame her. He's not only pulled her so close she can't move, but with his free hand he's grabbed her chin and pulled her head towards him. It looks uncomfortable. It's uncomfortable to watch.

And I'm getting pissed. Asshole is lucky my brothers are not here. They have much shorter fuses than I do.

"My friend," Dimitri starts to say while Charleigh looks at me with begging eyes, "in the spirit of goodwill, you know, as a gesture, so to speak, you Alekseevs will give me this lovely lady for the night. Okay Niko?"

Charleigh's eyes bulge and her one arm that is not pinned by Dimitri starts to flap. She's reaching for me.

But I don't move. This will be resolved with words.

Until it can't.

"Dimitri, there's no way in hell you will ever spend a minute of time with this woman," I say through a huge, fake-ass smile.

His only reaction is a slight twitch of his left eye. "Oh, Niko. You know it's time for us to become… good friends. No more rivalry. Think how much the *Pakhan* will like that."

Yes, the *Pakhan* wants peace between us. For old insults to be set aside. But he's a reasonable man and does not expect peace at any cost. Even if he did, Dimitri would still never get his fucking hands on Charleigh.

In fact, his arm around her is starting to bug me. Really bad.

I reach for her free arm, the one that's flailing toward me, and yank her so fast she spins out of Dimitri's arm and right into mine. In spite of herself, she squeals from the fast move, and for a moment I can imagine I know what she sounds like when she's happy.

Would that I could hear that again...

I not only pull Charleigh into the crook of my arm, but to further secure herself, she wraps her arms around me, gripping my suit jacket in tight fists as if really anchoring herself.

Her hair smells nice. Recently washed, I guess. Her arms are thin but solid and she has me in quite the grip. I pull her tighter. I could encircle her with both arms, but I know to keep one free when dealing with a dick like Dimitri. You never know what a scumbag like him might try.

One of the first things I learned. Keep your shooting hand free.

I like having Charleigh cling to me, especially in front of this asshole. She feels good, nestled against me. Like she belongs. Like she fits. I slowly turn, directing her down the hall and toward my office, our backs fully turned on Dimitri as a big *fuck you*.

This is going to piss him off, which I am immensely enjoying.

"Niko," he calls after me. I debate ignoring him, but he is a member, and besides, it's so much fun to patronize him.

Charleigh and I turn. "Yes, Dimitri?" I ask with a huge smile.

He just smiles back. Without saying a word.

NIKO

When Charleigh and I get to my office, she exhales a deep breath. "That guy was creepy," she says. "I mean, there are lots of creeps here, but that one—" She glances up at me, realizing she just stuck her foot in her mouth, talking about club members.

I burst out laughing. Charleigh is puzzled for a moment, horrified by her slip-up, until it dawns on her I'm not only *not* insulted, but that I also think what she said is freaking hilarious. So raw. So innocent. So impulsive.

That's what feels nice. The impulsivity. I've not been around her for more than a few days and can already tell she doesn't worry about choosing her words carefully like most people I know. She's not of that world, where people say the wrong thing and end up on the wrong end of a gun. She has no idea anything like that even exists.

Another reason I'm drawn to her.

She's so… fresh.

"Here, Charleigh, have a seat," I say, gesturing toward a leather sofa once we're in my office.

I take the chair opposite. I want her to relax, maybe have a drink. Kick back and chat. I am guessing she's been on edge since my brothers and I showed up at her dad's place last week. We've tried to make her comfortable with lush accommodations and chef-prepared meals. But she'd rather not be here. I can't blame her. She's in a difficult position, having to save her father. I get it.

If Vadik or Kir find out I have such compassionate thoughts on my mind, they'll shit. They will not be happy.

Charleigh takes a long draw on the Perrier I gave her, after turning down something harder. "Niko," she says, "you're blond but your brothers are dark-haired."

She doesn't ask a question. She just states the obvious in a way that an answer is expected. Or at least hoped for.

To most people who bring this up, I offer nothing. It's not their business. I don't give a shit how curious they are. But Charleigh is a different story. I've lived betrayal, like she has. Maybe not on the same level, but it sticks with you. I can see it in her the same I see it in myself.

I start slowly. I am not accustomed to sharing my story. "The guys and I don't all have... the same father."

I take a deep breath. Fuck me. It's hard enough to spit those few words out. How the hell will I continue with the rest of the story?

"I see."

I nod, staring down at my fingers, now spread over my thighs.

I consider stopping. Sending Charleigh away to go do whatever she has to do, and getting back to work. Not thinking about anything else.

But I want to talk. I want her to know me just like I want to know her.

"For most of my childhood," I start, "I thought Grigory Alekseev was my father. But when I got to be twelve or so, my mother sat me down and told me I had a different dad than Vadik and Kir. A dad who was *not* Grigory Alekseev."

"Whoa," Charleigh says.

"It turned out," I continued, "my mother had an

affair with… well, it doesn't matter who. Anyway, I am the result of that. My real father wanted nothing to do with me, so Grigory adopted me."

I glance over at her, anticipating pity or disgust, that I'm the product of an illicit relationship. That I'm walking, living proof that my mother did not stay faithful to her husband, despite her marriage vows. That I'm a reminder to my family every day of my mother's fuck up.

Even though my philandering father deserved every bit of betrayal that came from her. And then some.

But double standards and all that.

Charleigh's look contains none of these things. She nods evenly. Without judgment. She knows there's nothing to gain from throwing sympathy at me. Nothing to be gained by trying to placate me.

She's a person with her own problems and knows everyone else has them too.

When I was born, fortunately for me—and my mother—Grigory stepped up to the plate, and just like my brothers, treated me like a full member of the family from day one. There was never a moment in my life they let me feel like an outsider. And for that, I will be unwaveringly loyal to them until my death.

That made losing Grigory that much harder. He'll never get to see what I can accomplish.

Which makes me hate Dimitri Yegorov that much more. He stole the father I owed everything to.

Everything.

CHAPTER TWENTY-THREE

CHARLEIGH

I slouch into Niko's deep, well-worn leather sofa, thrilled to be off my feet after three hours of serving drinks in the club lounge, and kick off the stripper high heels Dominika makes me wear. I rub some circulation back into my cramped toes, and don't care if it's an inappropriate thing to do in front of Niko.

I have no idea what sort of rules of decorum they have here, but I am guessing when I break them, someone will let me know. I mean, if they don't want me rubbing my feet in front of them, they shouldn't make me wear these shoes.

But Niko says nothing, just watches, the corner of his mouth turned up like he's amused or something.

His office is beautiful, paneled in the dark wood I've seen all over the club, clearly some expensive decorator's idea of masculine décor. The built-in book shelves are fully loaded and not with tattered paperbacks like we have at my house. These are serious books with dark covers and gold lettering running down the spines. I'd like to go over to see what Niko has on offer but the books are probably just for show.

They can dress this place up any way they like, but it doesn't hide who these guys really are.

I reach for one of the sofa's throw pillows to pull into my lap to cover my thighs. The short skirt they gave me doesn't leave much to the imagination, and when I sit, I'm pretty much exposed for the world to see. But I need to play it cool instead of hiding behind a pillow, so I just pretend to stretch. I won't let them know they have me uncomfortable. That I have no idea what's around the next corner, and that I'm scared shitless. That I know these aren't nice people, and that they wouldn't hesitate to eat me for lunch.

Especially that Dominika. The woman is a witch, plain and simple. She looks like one with that hair piled high and makeup applied with a spatula, she sounds like one with her high-pitched voice and Russian accent, and she acts like one, screaming at people and ordering them all over the place.

The only time she acts like a normal human being, I've noticed, is when she's with guests, or the brothers, Vadik, Kir, or Niko.

What's interesting, though, is that I was not in the club twenty-four hours before I grasped how much she clearly dislikes them, in spite of smiling to their faces. It could hardly be more obvious. She knows she has to watch herself around them, though. Defer to them. Let them remain in charge. As insincere as all that is.

Maybe I could learn something from her. This fake-compliance is a survival tactic. And I'd like to survive.

"I'm having a drink," Niko says, getting up.

Jesus. People here drink around the clock. While I'm not sure what time it is—I don't see any clocks and the windows in Niko's office are darkened—I figure it's noon-ish. So yes, I'd love a drink. And I don't drink. I want to forget where I am, and stop thinking and worrying about what lies ahead. But I have to keep my wits about me. Stay sharp. Look for opportunities to get the hell out.

Leaving will probably mean the worst for my father. But how far does my loyalty, my obligation extend to a man willing to use me to alleviate his problems? And what if my younger sister, Evie, is next in line, next time Pops messes up? If I find a way to leave—I mean *when*—she's got to come with me.

I force a polite smile. "I'll have another water. Thank you, Niko."

He looks at me approvingly as if this is some kind of test, and reaches into a small fridge for another Perrier. He twists the cap off and hands it to me.

Of course this is a test. Everything is a test. They are constantly watching me, trying to figure me out just like I am trying to figure them out. We have conflicting objectives, and we both want to win. Problem is, they are pros at this and I don't know shit.

When Niko passes me my water, his fingers brush mine. He holds them there for a moment, both our hands on the green bottle, and strangely, like the time he stroked my hair in the hallway, his touch is comforting.

Good god.

The man made me sign a contract to agree to essentially being kidnapped, and I like the way his fingers feel on mine?

What is wrong with me?

And what is with this place?

They give me a beautiful room and nice food as if I'm some sort of important guest. Then, they subject me to Dominika's hellish orientation, including painfully tearing out all my pubic hair, and make me walk around half-naked in stripper heels serving cocktails at nine in the morning to a bunch of gross old pervs. I get stopped in the hallway by some greasy criminal, and Niko whisks me away to his plush office, smiling his handsome smile and giving me fancy bottled water. Not all prisons have bars, as the saying goes.

If these people are trying to fuck with me, they are doing a great job. I'm completely off-balance.

Who do I trust?

What's coming next?

Will I have the chance to get the hell out? And if so, where do I go?

CHAPTER TWENTY-FOUR

CHARLEIGH

Niko's office door flies open, startling us both. I drop my Perrier bottle, and it tumbles to the plush carpet below, where it begins to empty.

I gasp and snatch it up as fast as I can.

Vadik looks between the two of us and scowls. My heart jumps into my throat. Have I done something wrong?

But Niko is unfazed and without hesitation, crosses the room in two long steps and grabs a cloth napkin from the bar cart. I move my knees aside to make room as he dabs at the wet carpet next to my stocking feet.

And hell if he doesn't smell nice. With him crouched so close, I watch a lock of blond hair fall onto his forehead, and have a strong urge to push it off his face. I sit on my hands to resist the temptation, and he finally scrapes it back with his own free hand.

What the hell is wrong with me? These guys are keeping me here basically against my will. I say basically, because I signed that damn contract, but what choice did I have? It was me or Pops.

Or Evie, God forbid.

Urges aside, I am not here to be Niko's friend, nor his brothers. No, I'm here to 'work,' whatever the hell that entails. So far, it means serving cocktails to creepy, handsy men, and avoiding slimy trouble-makers in the corridor.

Oh, and trying not to piss off the mercurial Dominika.

Dream job, yo.

What a hellhole I've fallen into.

Vadik places a hand on my bare shoulder. It's warm and soothing, and once again I'm cursing myself for thinking it could be anything more than it actually is.

These guys don't give a rat's ass about you, idiot.

He gives me a light squeeze. It's neither sexual nor inappropriate. Just kind of... friendly. "Charleigh, it's time for lunch. We'd like for you to join us."

There they go again with the being nice bullshit.

But I know it's just a matter of time before the other shoe drops. I've watched enough crime drama to know I'm being groomed. They make you think you're special, that they are there for you, and that you're safe. Then one day it all blows up. They do something horrible, worse than you could ever imagine. And you're surprised because you didn't see it coming through the flattery.

God help me when that happens. Because I know it will.

My feet are happy to have had the little break they did while I chilled on Niko's sofa, but when I pull my shoes back on and get to my feet, they silently start to scream again. Vadik gestures toward the door and both brothers allow me to pass first, as if they are real gentlemen or something.

Gentlemen who are ready to off my father at a moment's notice.

And as I step into the dimly lit hallway, trying my best not to limp, who do I nearly run smack into but Dimitri. Again.

This should be interesting.

He smiles, his yellow teeth failing to hide a waft of his cigarette breath, and my head snaps back in involuntary disgust. With more presence of mind, something I clearly need to work on, I could hide my revulsion.

"Well, if it isn't my pretty new friend, Charleigh," he booms, grabbing my hand before I can think to move out of his reach.

I back into the wall behind me, anyway.

And what does he do, but move closer.

Which, with a glance in their direction, makes Vadik and Niko unhappy.

Correction. *Very* unhappy.

There's some serious history here, and it isn't pretty.

Niko takes a step toward him. "Dimitri, I told you hands off," he growls.

Vadik looks among the three of us, quickly assessing what's going down. It doesn't take him long.

He smooths his hand over his shaved head, a casual, innocuous gesture, I can tell intended to keep the situation calm. Which means the situation probably won't remain calm.

I'm fascinated, bizarrely enjoying my front row seat, and at the same time wishing I were anywhere else on Earth at the moment.

"Dimitri, did my brother have a talk with you about Charleigh?" Vadik asks with a pleasant smile.

These guys are good. Like, Academy Award good.

And Dimitri, either stupid or masterfully antagonistic, waves him off like an annoying fly. "Oh,

Vadik, everything is fine. Niko is just a little… *protective* of your latest girl."

While new to this shitshow, even I can see that Dimitri's pushing his luck, probably on purpose, to get a rise from the guys. And to further double down, he pulls me close with a tight arm around my shoulder.

Again.

Talk about poking a bear. The man's crazy. And he clearly has something up his sleeve.

My mouth grows dry when Vadik steps closer to Dimitri, getting in his face, where I'm perfectly situated in the line of fire. I gently twist to get out of his grip, but he doesn't budge.

"Let her go," Vadik warns, his voice taking a warning edge. Close up, I can see tiny lines between his eyebrows, lines I'm pretty sure indicate his current mood.

Which is not happy.

Dimitri laughs. Because of course. He knows exactly how to push the brothers' buttons. These grievances are old. Longstanding. And infinitely deep.

And even when it looks like they're all about to come to blows, I still can't free myself. That does not bode well. I've seen a few fistfights in my day, and know the best thing is to get as far away from them as possible.

Niko takes up position next to his brother. "Vad, Dimitri here is under the impression he's somehow entitled to Charleigh. I told him otherwise, but for some reason the message hasn't sunk into his vodka-addled brain."

With all of them in an angry standoff, I nervously look from one to the other. If anyone loses his shit, I will end up with a black eye, broken nose, or worse.

I clear my throat quietly. Maybe I can attract their attention. They'll realize they need to get me out of the way. "Hey, guys, do you mind if I—"

But I stop. Even though I am intentional and confident in my tone, it is clear my appeal will do no good. I'm standing right before them, but it's like I'm not even there. As if I'm invisible. The expressions on their faces, like angry bulls, tell me they won't hear anything I have to say. While the conflict of the moment is about me on one level, it's anything but. These guys could be fighting over a cookie and would be just as threatening, vying for the position of top dog, remembering nothing but past insults, grievances, and betrayals.

I'm just an excuse for another thing to fight over.

It's not about me. Not at all.

The grin on Dimitri's face starts to falter, and I

sense things are getting more serious. His grip on me loosens and I quickly step out of the way. Which is not to say I relinquish my front row seat. On no, I'm not doing that. The more I learn about these guys and their operations, the better off I'll be at understanding what I'm up against.

And that will inform how I respond to things. It's all about self-preservation now. Nothing more. If these guys have the bitter, long-standing rift they appear to, I will find a way to exploit it.

CHAPTER TWENTY-FIVE

Charleigh

Like I'm some sort of masterful criminal strategist.

What a joke. If my bookkeeping instructor could see me now.

"This club," Dimitri finally says, spraying his rank saliva, "wouldn't exist without the largesse of *my father*. Your family would still be pushing shitty black-market vodka like they were when they got off the fucking boat. You'd be nobodies just like you were when your father first came from Russia." He scoffs, inches from their faces, with no concern for consequences. After all, he's outnumbered, his posse nowhere in sight.

Vadik widens his stance and pulls himself to full height. He's already taller than Dimitri, but this is what animals do when they fight. Make themselves as large as possible.

Dimitri remains unfazed. At least on the outside.

"Get the fuck out," Vadik says quietly and evenly, in the same tone as if he were asking if it might rain tomorrow.

Dimitri's mouth twitches, but that's the only part of him that moves. "Vadik, need I remind you that the truce between our families is fragile at best? You, my friend, need to be on your best behavior. Because I can take you down. I can take away everything you have and leave you with less than nothing. Like your family was before the time my father took pity on yours. He had to teach your father everything before he was finally able to stand on his own two feet. He had to *wipe your father's fucking ass.*"

Dimitri delivers a masterful smirk, one that could easily be wiped off his face, along with his gross teeth, with one big Alekseev hand. And yet he doesn't look worried.

Who has the power here? It's impossible to tell.

Maybe that's the reason for the conflict.

I take a couple steps back and then another for good measure. While I want to witness what's going on, I have a feeling it's going to get violent. And I do not plan to get stuck in the middle of flying fists.

Still, my heart is pounding.

For once, I wish Dominika would happen by.

Vadik bares his teeth when he speaks. "Dimitri, our debt to your family has been repaid many times over. It is long-erased. We owe you nothing except maybe a swift kick in the ass for showing up here and making trouble. You need to accept that times are different now, and that you, to put it simply, are no longer relevant, if you ever were. Further, you know there is no truce between our families. There never will be. You're only allowed in here as a member who spends a lot of money."

"And we're happy to take your money, Dimitri," Niko adds. "Just because the *Pakhan* has forbidden us to declare war on you, doesn't mean we're friends. There is no peace between us. There never will be."

Vadik nods slowly. "The absence of war does not indicate a truce."

The guys might not call this face-off a war, but it sure seems like one to me. Dimitri, perhaps defeated in this latest battle, turns on his heel and leaves, heading straight for the elevator, alone, defeated, and muttering under his breath.

He says nothing more, doesn't look back, just presses the elevator button and gets inside when the doors open.

After they close, I take a deep breath. I know this isn't the end of whatever these guys have going on, their protracted grievances, but for the moment, things go back to calm and quiet.

"So, anybody hungry?" Vadik asks with a smile when my growling stomach gives me away.

I played it safe as a fly on the wall during the brothers' exchange with Dimitri. But I am a fly no more as they turn their focus to me, smiling, leading the way to lunch.

"Glad he's gone," I say once we're in the dining room, taking my chances on bringing up a sore subject.

I need to find out where I stand with all that's happening. Gather whatever information I can.

Find the guys' Achilles heel, so to speak.

If they think I'm just going to sit around and see what comes my way, they are completely insane.

But until I find a way to save myself, I'll plow through the crap they throw my way with a pleasant little smile. That way, when I do make my move, they'll be caught completely unaware.

At least, that's what I'm banking on.

CHAPTER TWENTY-SIX

VADIK

"Look who it is," my brother says, rising from the dining table to pull out Charleigh's chair. "I understand you've built quite the fan club."

Tossing her hair with a laugh, she lets Kir push her chair in. She places her napkin on her lap to cover the fact that her skirt is ridiculously short and pulls her shoulders back like she runs around in strapless tops all the time.

She's playing like she's cool with everything happening around her, but she's not fooling anyone. Well, maybe my smitten younger brothers, but I know there's no way anyone like this girl adjusts to our world inside of a few days of being exposed to it.

No matter the sumptuous digs and good food we've plied her with.

It will take time for her to comprehend all that's going on around her. And to accept what comes her way.

With the four of us at the table, I holler for Chef, who begins to serve our lunch.

We start with a tasty little *amuse-bouche* shot glass of some sort of delicious soup, followed by a delicious pan-seared salmon and a tangy frisée salad. It's the perfect midday meal, like Chef always makes for us, and it will leave me satisfied, but not overly full.

I don't like to overeat at lunch. It messes up the rest of my day. Actually, I don't even like fancy meals like ones that include an *amuse-bouche*, but when Papa arrived from Russia, he fell in love with a famous French restaurant that served them. Thereafter, he required Chef to serve one at every meal, except breakfast, of course.

They're a lot of work for one bite of food, and personally, I'd be happy with a turkey sandwich for lunch, but that's just me.

"Who is this Dimitri guy? What's his deal?" Charleigh asks. Her voice is casual, like she's asking what time it is.

But her intent is not.

Got to give her credit for persistence. The first time she tried to initiate a conversation about him, none of us responded. I figure she got the message, not to ask too many questions. After all, we invited her to lunch to get to know her better, not the other way around.

But when she brings it up again, I see she either didn't read between the lines, or she did and doesn't care. I'm not sure what she's on about—whether she's trying to provoke us guys or is just genuinely curious about the asshole.

I decide to give her the benefit of the doubt. If she has questions, she'll get answers. Although she might not like what she hears.

But that's on her.

I glance her way and see she's finished her entire lunch in the time it's taken my brothers and me to barely eat half of ours. She must have been starving. I make a mental note to talk to Chef about making sure she's well-fed. If left to Dominika, the girl will be lucky to get prison rations.

Niko notices how fast she cleaned her plate too. "Enjoy your lunch, Charleigh?" he asks.

Her eyes fall closed. "Oh my god. It was amazing. I've only ever had salmon one other time before and it wasn't very good. This was amazing and I was starving."

As soon as she says that, her hand flies to her mouth, like she didn't mean to admit to her hunger.

Niko doesn't like that. "God, Charleigh, sounds

like we haven't been feeding you enough. We won't let that happen again."

That's Niko. Always looking out for the wounded birds.

But hell, I don't want her hungry, either. She's worth a lot to us guys—to the entire club—and it won't do to leave her underfed.

"Anytime you want anything to eat, Charleigh," Niko continues, "just holler. Chef can fix you something on a moment's notice. Anything you want. Okay?"

She nods gratefully and takes a pretend sip of her wine.

Interesting.

I am about to correct Niko, point out to him that no one gets free rein of the kitchen, but decide not to shit on his moment of kindness. For the first time since we sat for lunch, Charleigh seems genuinely relaxed. Not worried about what's around the next corner.

She would do well not to get *too* relaxed. But it's not the time to bring that up.

"Charleigh, in answer to your question, Dimitri's father and ours were business partners. They opened this club together as well as many of the other businesses that we run to this day. Dimitri's dad, when he died, left the club and everything to our dad rather than his son. You see, Dimitri is somewhat of a bum. Spends his father's money jetting around the world like a general party boy."

That's putting it kindly. The guy is a useless dirtbag of the first degree.

Charleigh looks at me, her eyes wide. "I take it he didn't like that too much."

I press my lips together and nod. Understatement of the century. The guy's resentment is legendary. But it's of his own doing. There's no one else to blame.

Kir continues. "You're right. Not only didn't he like it one bit, his obsession with being passed over has caused him to… make some bad decisions over the years."

"Like murdering our parents," I say.

CHAPTER TWENTY-SEVEN

The room is silent. Not even a fork clangs against a plate.

"He was responsible for your parents' death?" Charleigh whispers, swallowing hard.

I hesitate, never sure I want to talk about this. It's been two years, but it still feels like yesterday. I brought it up, though, so I'll finish the story. "We haven't proven he was behind it yet. But we've always been certain it was him."

"It's just a matter of time, though. Someday he'll trip up, maybe admit to it, maybe not, but he'll pay," Kir adds, looking across the room with a blank stare. "The worst of it is that our dad felt sorry for Dimitri and to honor his longtime friend, tried to look after him once his father passed. Papa was so kind to him.

Both our parents were. And look at how they were treated in the end…"

Kir stops. There's really not much more to say.

My jaw twinges, and I realize I've been grinding my teeth. Something I never did before my parents were killed.

"Charleigh, stay away from that guy. He's a predator. He comes near you, tell us," Niko says.

She nods silently, her eyes wide.

Yeah, she's in a totally new world now. She might not see what's ahead, but she sure as hell knows it's not going to be like anything she's ever known.

Her eyes get glossy and her nose starts to pink. She sniffles hard and clears her throat, chasing away the threatening tears. Her relaxed demeanor of a few minutes ago has all but faded. "What happened, when your parents died?" she asks quietly. "The ones I was at the funeral for? Something about a fire?"

Again, the room's silent except for Chef's assistant, who clears our plates.

"Yes. There was a fire. Whoever set it targeted the room where our parents were sleeping. It spread so fast they didn't even make it to the bedroom door when they tried to escape," I say matter-of-factly, forcing myself to breathe.

In, out, in, out.

The fire was no doubt the work of a professional.

Dimitri didn't do it himself. He's far too stupid to pull off anything like that. I'm certain he hired someone. Someone who knew just what they were doing.

"That's where I first saw you," I say, looking straight at Charleigh. "Your father came to pay his respects at the funeral. You were on the other side of the room."

What a time that was. Visitors, calls, flowers. Meetings with lawyers, sorting out the will. And then there was the food people sent. So much, it was ridiculous. We did not eat a single bite of it. Whoever got rid of our parents might want to get rid of my brothers and me, next.

Looking down at her hands, Charleigh shakes her head. "I'm so sorry."

She might not specifically recall me from that day, but I do her, in a simple black dress and scuffed shoes. She was out of place, on one hand, not dressed as nicely as the rest of the crowd pouring through the receiving line. But she was also one of the few who wasn't there with her hand out, so to speak. She wasn't asking for anything, like so many others were.

Kir rolls his shoulders and his neck cracks loudly. "After Papa died, our incompetent uncle took over the club. And now *he's* gone."

"Gone?" Charleigh asks. "Like deceased, gone?"

If only.

"Oh no," Niko snickers. "He fled the country on tax evasion charges. We don't know where he is. But he left us a mess to clean up. He made off with a lot of the club's cash, so we're trying to put the place back together, so to speak."

Charleigh's lips press together. It's dawning on her that she's part of this rebuilding too. So to speak.

Actually, she's a *huge* part of it.

I pour a second glass of wine, carefully paired with the meal by Chef—another fancy requirement of Papa's that's still in practice for some inane reason. I rarely have more than one drink at lunch, but after our run in earlier with the scumbag Dimitri, I figure I've earned a bonus one. My brothers clearly feel the same and gesture for me to top them off. Charleigh is the only one who took no more than a taste of hers. She thinks this goes unnoticed, but it does not, at least not by me. I miss nothing. Knowing what the hell is going on around me at all times is part of what's made me successful. Kept me alive.

She might think she's smart by not drinking. Keeping her wits about her, as if that might benefit her in some way. But she's not smarter than my brothers and me. Few people are.

After learning more about our lives than she

probably bargained for in one sitting, she looks small at our table, her shoulders slumped, her arms crossed. A defensive posture if ever there was one.

I want to take her in my arms.

Fuck all. This isn't like me. Not one bit.

But I'm willing to take a chance. "Charleigh, come over here, please," I say, patting my thigh.

I'm not sure how she'll react to this, but I have to say, she's just so fetching across the table, whether she's closed off or not.

Watching her has left me with a slight midday hard-on that I need to get under control.

Or not.

She looks around, first at my brothers and me, like she's not sure whether I'm serious. Then, to my surprise, she shrugs, gets to her feet, and makes her way over to my side of the table, slightly wobbly in the high heels she's still not particularly graceful in.

I push my chair out and take her onto my lap. While she's tall, she feels small in my arms, I suppose because she's on the skinny side. She folds herself into me and presses her head to my chest, eyes closed.

To say I'm surprised is an understatement. But I'm pretty sure she does little that's not premeditated, and that she thinks she's pulling one over on me. That's okay, though. We're going to have a little fun.

I inhale her scent, which stirs something unfamiliar in me. I'm used to women being perfumed to the ends of their hair, overly made up, and eager to please because they expect something in return.

Charleigh might learn to think like that someday. But for now, in her innocence, she has no idea how her beauty can be used as currency. She still believes in merit. Getting ahead with honest hard work. Without cheating or taking shortcuts. Acting with honor. And integrity.

So naïve.

I push her thick hair aside, baring her skin, and run a finger over the warm crook of her neck. In spite of whatever she might have up her sleeve, she nestles deeper into my arms and emits a sigh. She's happy to accept a little comfort, even if it is from an insincere bastard like me. My brothers watch from the other side of the table with great curiosity, wondering where this is going.

Just like I know they have the hots for her, they now know I do, too.

CHAPTER TWENTY-EIGHT

VADIK

When my stroke moves from her neck to her shoulder, I continue down her long, graceful arm, leaving a trail of goosebumps, and end up on her thigh. The hem of her short skirt and the lacy top of her stocking expose a nice swath of skin that immediately warms under my touch. I ease my fingers to her inner thigh, and begin to work her leg, previously plastered to the one next to it, open a couple inches.

While I'm doing this, I clasp her chin with my free hand and maneuver her closer to my lips until I can taste the soft, fragrant skin of her neck.

She stiffens for a moment when I pull her leg away from the one next to it, but when I leave a trail of kisses on her neck, she relaxes back into me.

I wonder how often our pretty girl masturbates. And how she does it. Is she a lay on her stomach type, working her hand down between her legs? Or is she a hump the pillow type? Maybe she lays on her back with her legs pressed tightly together to enhance the sensation. Does she fuck herself with her hand? Or just play with her clit until she comes?

I want to know all this and more. And I will find out, given the time.

But until that happens, I want to bring our girl some pleasure.

I graze my fingertips across the crotch of her panties and she shudders. She begins to pull her legs back together, but I hold them in place.

"Wh… what are you doing?" she asks in a dreamy voice, pushing against the hand holding her legs open.

"Charleigh," I whisper, "what are *you* doing? Are you telling me to *stop*? Are you telling me *no*?"

Her eyes flutter open like she's suddenly awake. "I… I don't know," she says, quivering.

"Well, baby, I can tell you one thing, and it's that *no* is no longer part of your vocabulary."

I wedge a knee between her legs to hold them apart and return my fingers to the thin fabric covering her pussy.

"Wh… what?" she gasps.

"You are here for the pleasures of the flesh. I will enjoy you. My brothers will enjoy you. And others will too."

She clearly doesn't find this to be good news and stiffens in my arms, even pressing slightly against me as if she wants to go. But my fingers, intertwined with her hair, clamp down in a tight grip and hold her in place. My other hand continues to stroke the outside of her panties, stretched tightly over what I'm guessing is bare flesh, now that she's benefitted from our spa services. The button of her clit stiffens, joining the party.

"Ahhhh…" she says softly, unconsciously pressing into my hand by shifting her hips.

I intensify my strokes, still outside her panties, letting my fingers slide to the hollow spot between her lips where the most heat emanates. The fabric quickly soaks through with her excitement, and her head drops back on my shoulder as she no longer has the urge to get away. She either is unaware of how my brothers are watching her so intently, or she doesn't care. I'm not sure which.

But I see them shift in their seats, and when I catch their gaze, they nod back at me, approving my actions, happy to see our lovely guest enjoying herself.

Gesturing with his chin, my brother Kir suggests

he wants to see more. I ease a finger inside the elastic leg of Charleigh's panties until I touch her hot, bare skin, and my god, I slide through her juices and they feel like liquid gold, that's how precious it all is.

She squirms slightly in my arms, and I bring my wet finger to my mouth like a starving man. She tastes heavenly, like I knew she would, and my dick fully hardens underneath where her bottom is resting.

It hurts but also feels good, which is just how I like it.

I haven't come in my pants since I was a horny teenager, but this might be the day that happens again. If so, I don't give a damn. I shift in my chair to position our girl more fully over my erection, positioning my cock more or less between her ass cheeks.

Unable to hold back any longer, I fully pull aside the crotch of her panties in view of my brothers, who wear approving grins, and open her pussy lips for their viewing pleasure.

God knows I'd like to take her, lay her on the table before us, push her knees to her chest, and drive my cock into her soaked virgin hole.

But I won't. I won't take her virginity, as much as I want it with every fiber of my being. And in order not to defile her with my fingers, I only insert the very tips of them so as not to break her precious barrier. I want to give her pleasure, I want to make her feel as good as she deserves, so I drag some of her juices further, until I meet the crack of her ass and her tight little rosebud.

I'm in fucking agony, dry humping her bum, but when I reach her asshole and circle a wet finger around her tight ring, I feel her open a little, and that's when I groan. I don't come, I'm old enough to fucking control myself, but I promise myself her ass when the time is right.

Why don't more American girls hold on to their virginity? Don't they know its worth? The value is inestimable, and if I were to take Charleigh's that would be a colossal waste.

And just when I know it's time to excuse myself to go jerk off, Charleigh's breath quickens to a new pace and a long, low moan escapes her mouth. I get back to working her clit as she thrashes on my lap, and a glance at my brothers reveals them each rearranging their own erections.

Charleigh comes into my hand, her pussy releasing a flood of her excitement onto my trousers as she convulses lightly, clinging to my arms so hard she leaves nail marks. I don't mind. Not at all. Her hips buck lightly and her knees fall further apart, any previous modesty forgotten. She might not know it, but her body does—she needs this release like she needs the air around her.

When she begins to still, my brothers leave the room without her noticing, and I dab her with one of the cloth napkins left from lunch.

I want more from this girl. But she's not mine. She's not intended for any of the Alekseev brothers. Unless there's a change of plans. A major change of plans.

CHAPTER TWENTY-NINE

CHARLEIGH

"How's it going?"

I spot Stacey, the girl who was nice to me when I was going through what I guess I could call my 'initiation.' She looks at me with a sort of kind curiosity. Not saying she can help me with my predicament, but that she does feel for me, regardless. I'm desperate for a friend, an ally. Will she be this, for me?

I wonder what her 'situation' is.

Even though her question, asking me how I am, is innocent and would be polite in normal circumstances, given my bizarre alternative reality—I'm tempted to scream at her.

How the fuck do you think it's going? I want to

holler with every bit of fury and helplessness I possess.

But I don't. I keep my angry words to myself.

Although that doesn't mean my emotions are not written all over my face.

She nods and quickly looks away, back at the brightly lit makeup mirror, and continues applying her eyeliner. "Yeah. I figured as much," she says in response to my silence.

"Why are you here? Are you being held against your will?" I ask.

She glances over at me, her brows furrowed like my question confuses her. "Aren't we all here against our will, on some level?"

She has a point.

Taking a magazine, she fans it over her face, presumably to dry the mascara she's applied. She moves to the seat next to mine at the long table covered with all sorts of makeup, wigs, cheap costume jewelry, and other trappings of this strange profession that's been chosen for me.

"Look, Charleigh, is it?" she asks.

I nod.

"I can walk out of here any time I want. But I don't. I don't because I can't, when it comes down to it. I need to earn a living to support myself and my kid. There's no baby daddy in the picture. You know that old story, told from the beginning of freaking time. And I earn more here than I would anywhere else. So yeah, I'm stuck. I can leave, but I can't leave, if you know what I mean. You could probably leave too, if you want. It might not be recommended. I mean, I don't know a damn thing about you. But if this place is that bad for you, just bail."

Her eyes are wide, sincere in a way that shocks me, it's so unexpected. How does someone so open and honest end up in this world? And remain in it?

I feel a lump growing in my throat, and I swallow it down, hard. My voice cracks anyway. "Fact is, Stacey, I *can't* leave. I mean, I guess I could, but some very bad things will happen."

As time has passed, I'm less concerned about my father. My younger sister Evie, on the other hand, is never far from my thoughts in spite of the teenage rebellion that has her acting like she's possessed by the devil.

"Oh. Right," Stacey says, looking back in the mirror to avoid my gaze. She knows something.

"*What?*" I ask. I need her to tell me everything she knows. If I can get her to.

She clasps her hands in her lap and looks down at them. "Well, if you can't leave, like there's just no way, that means… that means they have special plans for you."

It feels like someone is punching me in the gut. But I inch closer to her so she senses my desperation, and I lower my voice. "Special plans? What are *special plans*? Are they going to… make me a stripper or something?"

Stacey giggles. "Oh no. There's nothing special about *that*. Just look at me. I strip here five, six days a week. That's just a regular gig for this club. They have other… placements—"

She gasps as the dressing room door violently bangs open, and Dominika charges in, her bosom pushed up so high, the tops of her breasts jiggle as she storms toward us.

Stacey jumps to her feet.

"And what are you two ladies whispering about?" Dominika demands, propping her butt on the table right next to me.

All I can focus on is her overpowering perfume. It wouldn't be so bad if she didn't overdo it, but this isn't the kind of woman who embraces subtlety.

"Nothing, Dominika," Stacey says in a shaky voice. "We're just… chatting. You know."

I nod. "Stacey was showing me how she does her… makeup. I was thinking I ought to get good at it."

Dominika looks between the two of us and rolls her eyes. "Good. We can't have you going around like such a plain Jane all the time, can we?" Her head drops back and she cackles with her mouth open, revealing the gaps where she's missing teeth.

She glances at her watch and glares at Stacey. "You were supposed to be on three minutes ago. Stop flapping your gums and get to work," she snaps.

Stacey high-tails it out of the room and Dominika turns her attention to me. I shudder to think what she wants.

"You," she starts, "come with me. It's time for your exam."

CHAPTER THIRTY

Charleigh

Oh my god. Is this really happening? I hoped she was just cruelly joking.

I also hoped I'd earned… *something* from lunch's sexy time. Maybe a privilege of some sort for submitting to Vadik's wandering hands and his brothers' wandering eyes. Guess not.

But to be honest, I didn't play along because I was trying to gain any sort of favor. The truth is, I enjoyed it. I never thought of myself as an exhibitionist, but those guys watching me, while I should have been embarrassed and ashamed, somehow egged me on. I wanted more.

So many levels of fucked up.

"C'mon," Dominika says, opening the dressing room door.

I follow her to the 'spa,' where they gave me that hideously painful waxing, and sit on the edge of the exam table.

"Take your panties off and lay back. Put your feet on the edge of the table. Scoot down more."

I wrestle myself into position, completely exposed, and shut my eyes tightly in anticipation of what's next.

The door opens and Dominika calls out. "Doctor. You can come in now."

Oh god.

"Hello, Charleigh."

I open my eyes to see a pockmarked old man set his bag down next to the table. He doesn't even glance my way as he pulls on a white coat and exam gloves and withdraws a syringe from his bag, exposing the top of his combed-over scalp to me. With a couple taps on my inner arm, he withdraws a small vial of blood. Dominika stands back, her arms crossed, supervising.

He drops the vial into some sort of container and moves to the end of the table where my legs are splayed open. He removes his gloves, and I watch a small smile grow on his face as he opens and pokes around my pussy lips with his bare, rough fingers, teasing my clit until I want to die of shame.

"What are you doing? This is not what's done in an exam—"

But Dominika presses my arm where the blood was just withdrawn and the pain shuts me up.

"Almost done, Charleigh. Now try to relax," he says, his voice thick. "She's nice and responsive, Dominika. You've done well here."

She just grunts.

"Ooof," I groan as he pushes two fingers into my vagina, stopping when he meets resistance. It doesn't feel good.

Nothing like what Vadik did the day before.

"Wow," he says, withdrawing his fingers and turning to Dominika. "She's the real thing. You know how rare that is?"

They continue talking about me like I'm not even there, like I'm nothing more than a hymen and a clitoris, so I sit up on the table and pull my legs together.

"I'll be back to you with the blood results in a couple days, but I don't think we'll find any surprises. Let me know if you need help with the photos. You know that's one of my weaknesses," he says with a watery chuckle.

Photos? What the fuck?

Dominika pats him on the back as he heads to the door. She closes it after him.

"Now that wasn't so bad, was it?" she asks.

She doesn't give me a chance to answer, not that I would.

"Now, let's get you to work."

CHAPTER THIRTY-ONE

CHARLEIGH

Back in my room after what seems like a marathon midday shift of shuttling back and forth between the bartender and club patrons, ensuring their glasses are always full of whatever beverage they require, I'm so tired I want to cry. I pull off the crazy stripper shoes I've been wobbling around in and rub my ankles, when the idea of a hot bath crosses my mind.

I sit on the edge of my huge tub, waiting for it to fill, and pull the sash on my plushy robe tighter. What a head-snapping contradiction the last couple days of my life have been.

I was basically felt up by someone who probably wasn't even a doctor, my asscheeks have been pinched, caressed, and smacked more times than I can count, and yet here I am living in this gorgeous suite, for lack of a better term, with the sort of bathroom that is only found in high-end décor magazines.

Then there are the guys. Aside from their initial threats when they took me from Pops's shop, they've treated me... like a princess. Well, a princess who works as a cocktail waitress. The hot lunchtime working-over Vadik gave me, which I have been thinking about every night before I go to bed, still blows my mind. It's like one of those ear-worm songs that you can't get out of your head.

Speaking of Pops's shop, Vadik returned my phone to me earlier in the day, and while I have missed a few calls, there is not a single one from my father.

Not a one.

Can't say I'm surprised.

There is a message from Evie, though, but I'll deal with that later. I need some time to think. Unless my father already filled her in, which I doubt, I have to be careful with what I tell her. He's probably too much of a chicken-shit to say anything, though. He knows how hard she'll come down on him. She might be young, but she's perceptive. When she doesn't see me around, she'll start asking questions.

There are five texts from my bookkeeping study-buddy, Luci. Ugh. I know exactly what she wants, and I have exactly no answers to give her. But I call her anyway.

"What the hell, dude?" she asks without saying hello.

I sigh. "I know. I'm sorry I've been so incommunicado."

"The exam is tomorrow!"

Like I could forget that. Like I haven't thought of my bookkeeping course every five minutes since I was spirited away from Dad's clusterfuck of a mess. Like I haven't wondered if all my hard work was for nothing, and whether the life I dreamt of for so long is now, forever, out of reach, all because of my father.

My voice cracks. "Luci, you go take it. Take the test. You get an A for us both. I don't know when I'll be back."

If ever.

I want to double over, the pain of giving up is so shattering. I was going to accomplish so much. I tried so hard.

"That's bullshit, Charleigh. Tell me where you are. I'll come get you right now."

And end up dead.

Not an option.

"Look, Lu, I love that you are on my side. I love

that we're twins in this journey to better ourselves. But I… am taking a break for now."

"Please, Charleigh, please tell me what's going on."

I am tempted to. I really am. But I know that will only put her in danger. So, for now, I am keeping my mouth shut.

"I can't say anything, Lu. Except I love you. And that I'll be in touch. Goodbye."

"Wait, Char—" she screams.

But I've hung up the call before I hear any more. I can't take the idea I'm letting her down, leaving her to finish on her own. We've held each other up, cheered each other on, and now I'm throwing her out there to do it on her own.

It's not like I have any choice, though.

I step into the steaming tub, which immediately works my sore legs. I swish the water around, having used shampoo as bubble bath, and pretend for a moment I'm a lady of leisure, entitled to such luxury on demand.

I try to force my thoughts back to my brief time with Vadik, his comforting, sensual touch, and block out the disgusting touch of that perv doctor, who probably jerked himself to relief the minute he got into his car. And just when I've closed my eyes to focus on the sweet-smelling water I'm soaking in, my phone vibrates on the edge of the tub.

I grab it before it tumbles into the water, having forgotten I'd left it there. I'm about to place it on the bathmat, turned over so I don't have to see Luci calling me again, when I find it's Evie's school.

Yes, the number for Evie's school is in my phone contacts, that's how often I talk to them.

I swipe the call open. "Hello? Hello?"

I hold my breath while I'm hanging out of the tub, dripping onto the floor. If Evie's gotten herself into some sort of mess, there's not a lot I can do in my current situation.

Shit, shit, shit.

"Miss Gates? This is Evie's principal."

I gulp. "Yes, I know. Is everything… all right?"

"Evie's gotten into another fight."

CHAPTER THIRTY-TWO

CHARLEIGH

I pull on the jeans and sneakers I arrived in, and sit on the edge of my bed, trying to think of what to do next.

I have to get to Evie's school. They won't let her go without either Pops or me picking her up, and they know better than to expect my father to do it.

I haven't seen the brothers all day, except for when Niko poked his head into the lounge and spotted me from across the room. He smiled, a fact not lost on the bartender and some of the guests, and after he left, I could swear I was treated with a little more respect. Or at least there was less ass-grabbing.

Aside from that, I know the brothers come and go, working their various businesses. They can't stay here in the club all day and night, even if it is their top priority of the moment. But I do hope to get some casual time with them later to learn more about what the hell I'm doing here.

I want to see them for other reasons, too. The sort of reasons that have been keeping me up at night, thinking naughty thoughts.

But my sister is my top priority. Everyone and everything else can go right to hell. Looking straight ahead, I walk out of my room to the elevator and head down to the ground floor, which I've not been on since the first day I arrived. I weave through some mingling guests until I push open the heavy door leading outside.

It slams behind me in a violent whoosh, and it occurs to me I have no way to get back in other than knocking. Or pounding.

How was that so easy? Can I just walk out anytime I want?

I know the answer to that. Yes, I can. But there are consequences. Ugly ones.

The brilliant daylight stuns me for a moment, and I realize I've only been exposed to artificial light for the last several days. I shield my eyes, squinting as I try to figure out which direction to head toward to get out of this forgotten industrial part of town and to my sister's school. I start walking as quickly but inconspicuously as possible while looking down at my phone to call an Uber.

That's when a large hand lands on my upper arm.

I turn to see Kir and my heart jumps into my throat. Dammit. What am I going to do now?

"Charleigh," he says, drawing out my name like I'm a bad little girl.

While he has me in his grip, his face is calm. Friendly, even. He's smiling the way you would if you've just run into a neighbor. His head is tilted, his longish hair pulled back tightly, and he's wearing some version of updated Ray-Bans.

If I passed him on the street, it would be all I could do not to stare. He looks like a genuinely nice, normal, although exceedingly handsome, guy. The kind most girls would be happy to date. Even bring home to Mom and Dad.

"Kir," I say, thinking fast. "Can you help me with something? I have a… family emergency."

Amusement crosses his face. "Um, sure, Charleigh. I'm happy to help," he says, not loosening his grip.

I look from where he's holding me to his face. "Kir. This is a real emergency. My sister is in trouble at school. I have no choice but to go to her."

He nods slowly, not buying a bit of it.

"Look, I need to get there ASAP and figure out

what's up. She's a… troubled kid. Things haven't been good for her since our mom died."

He should be able to relate to this, right?

And I guess he does, because his grip moves from my upper arm to my hand, which he takes, his fingers intertwining with mine. "All right. I'll take you."

Relief washes over me like a tidal wave and I can't believe my luck. I might get in trouble later, but I couldn't care less. There's no way that Kir—or anybody, really—can understand the depth of responsibility I feel toward Evie.

When our older sister left for New York, she made me swear I'd look out for the kid. I wasn't crazy about the idea because Evie's never been much more than a troublemaking brat, hanging with the wrong crowd, failing classes, and getting caught for boneheaded things like shoplifting candy. She needed some sort of guidance, though, and it wasn't going to come from our father. So, it fell to me.

As if she knows at this very moment I'm thinking of her, my phone vibrates with another call from her. I don't answer because she'll have too many questions I can't answer, and if she learns too much, she'll be here the next day, snooping around, getting involved, and generally making things worse for us both. So, I text her I'm on my way.

I turn to Kir after I've pulled my seatbelt on. "Are you taking me because you believe me? Or because you don't believe me?"

He thinks for a moment, before he puts the car into gear. "Maybe a little of both."

That's better than I expected.

He starts to drive, with me navigating, and it all just feels so normal. The sunroof of his Audi is open, the wind is blowing our hair, and he has the radio cranked up high. As the bass gets louder, he bops his head and slaps his thigh, and I think my life has never been this normal, even when it was normal.

CHAPTER THIRTY-THREE

Kir

Five minutes after arriving at Evie's high school, I have all those fuckers figured out.

Hell, I haven't been in a high school in years. I'm thirty-four years old, so it's been more than fifteen years. And yet everything looks the same, smells the same, hell, even *feels* the same.

While waiting for the principal to see Charleigh and me, I watch the kids crowd the hallways in between classes. Fashions might have changed, but it's impossible not to recognize the alpha pricks, who walk the halls with their heads so high in the air you can practically see inside their noses. Then, there are the kids they pick on, who walk looking down at their feet. And last, there's everyone in between, just trying to figure out life and get through the day.

And that's just high school. A bunch of kids. They've already figured out the hierarchy of life. If I had more time, I'd tell anyone who'd listen which ones would be successful, and which would be, ten years on, remembering high school as the best years of their life.

And then there's Evie, waiting outside the principal's office. What a sight. Hair dyed jet black, rings of messy black shit around her eyes, a pierced lip, and a scowl of epic proportion.

When I snagged Charleigh leaving the club earlier, I didn't doubt for a minute the story she told me, that she had to get her kid sister out of some sort of trouble at school. If she were really trying to escape, she'd have a much better story, first of all, and fought me a lot harder when I stopped her. No, her story was too real to be fake. Too mundane to have been invented.

Which interests me all the more.

Here's this woman, about to be offered up, basically, as a sacrificial lamb—unbeknownst to her— and she's worried about her little sister. In what world does that happen?

Not one I'm normally part of.

And yet her father is such a fucking loser. A

scumbag gambling addict who threw his beautiful, innocent daughter to the wolves to save his own ass, who can't even look after his younger one.

What a waste of flesh.

Do we really need him to repay us what he owes? Hell no. We have all the money we could spend in this lifetime and the next. But collecting debts is a matter of respect. If the people we do business with see us going soft, it would all be over.

So, in spite of the shitshow Charleigh's father created of her life, she still finds the time to be concerned about someone other than herself.

The woman continues to surprise me.

Like the day before when Vadik was having a go at her. I thought for sure she'd fight him off, but instead she kind of just fell into him, and let him make her feel good. Like she needed it.

The principal, a tired middle-aged woman with bleached hair, finally has time to see us. While I consider for a moment whether I should just wait outside, I figure what the hell, might as well watch how schools handle bad kids these days. They can't smack you across the face anymore, like they did at my Catholic school. These days they have to force kids into submission without the threat of pain hanging over their heads.

I'm not convinced that is a good thing.

"Thank you for calling me," Charleigh says to the principal. "Let's get this straightened out."

Shit. She's done this before.

I glance over at the brat in the corner who's causing Charleigh trouble just when she really doesn't need it, and the kid is glaring at me. Like if she had a sharp weapon in her hand, she'd just as soon stab me as walk down the hall to lunch. I stare back at her until she gets uncomfortable and looks away.

Little shit. I could straighten her right out.

After talking about the kid as if she's not even in the room, the principal sighs. What a shit job, dealing with crap like this day in and day out. No wonder the woman looks tired.

"Miss Gates, we can't keep making exceptions for your sister," the woman says, her lips tight.

Okay. I see what's going on. Charleigh might not, but I can read people. And this principal is a phony. She loves this shit. Punishing the baddies. She was probably one of the kids beaten down by the alphas back in the day. Finally getting revenge. On kids a quarter of her age.

But whatever. People are motivated by weird shit.

No one asks Evie what happened. For some reason, it's immaterial. Maybe she was justified in fighting? In my experience, people seldom throw a punch without good reason to.

But I keep my mouth shut. I have no horse in this race.

I'm tempted to tell Charleigh to let the brat go. That she needs to learn to fend for herself. Charleigh can't keep bailing her out. Hell, after the auction, she might be on the other side of the world, anyway. She won't be available for bullshit like this.

But she doesn't need to know any of this. She'll find out soon enough. In fact, if all goes according to plan, she could be gone this weekend.

CHAPTER THIRTY-FOUR

Kir

Kind of makes me sad. But business is business.

Hell, we have some crazy fuckers from Saudi Arabia coming in. They love nothing more than a pretty American girl to add to their collections of concubines to churn out baby after baby. And these guys pay top dollar.

I've even heard—never verified though, because how would I?—that they remove the women's clits so they can't enjoy sex. They just become baby-making machines.

Sick fucks, if you ask me. Who wants to fuck a corpse? Isn't it better when the woman enjoys herself? Guess these guys are not into a woman's pleasure. They're just cum dumpsters, as they call them. They collect women like they do exotic cars. But they treat the cars better.

When it comes down to it, are my brothers and I any better? We're just as fucking beastly as the next crazy bastard.

It's a shame Charleigh fell into our lives. She might have done well for herself otherwise. She's even mentioned something at one point about taking classes.

Those days are over, now.

"So, how'd your sister get so off track?" I ask once we're in the car, Charleigh having made some sort of deal with the principal where Evie promised to be a good girl.

I give the kid twenty-four hours before she fucks up again.

As we drive, it's not lost on me, the way she's looking out the window like she's soaking up scenery she may never see again.

Maybe she knows more than I realize, knows our plan for her. Or at least suspects it.

She lets out a long exhale, still spacing out on the landscape we're whizzing past. "My mom was murdered when I was ten. Evie was about six. She's been a mess ever since. In and out of trouble all the time. Stealing from the shop, my dad, fighting, running away. Pops threw in the towel. But I didn't. I can't. In honor of my mother."

I glance over at her. She's put her feet up on the dashboard and let her long hair whip out the car window. I could drive around all day like this with a pretty, dream-filled girl by my side.

Maybe I could just keep going. Drive till we run out of gas.

I nearly laugh out loud that that one. Sounds like some sad-sack fucking movie.

"Your mother was murdered?" I say. It's more of a statement than a question. But I want to know more.

Charleigh's attention snaps back. "Yeah. She was at the pawn shop and there was a hold up."

At that shitty place her old man runs? Someone held that place up and committed murder there? Why does her father still have the place open, for fuck's sake? If it were me, I'd shut it down and find something else to do. Leave town, too.

Gil Gates is an odd man.

"And… they just shot her?" I ask.

Something isn't right about this story.

A normal burglar doesn't just shoot people. They're usually way too pussy-ass for that sort of thing.

Charleigh nods. "Yup. The police investigated it and everything. The odd thing was, they didn't take anything, the robbers. Cops figured they got scared, shot my mom, and took off."

And there we have it. The 'police investigated.' How many times have I heard that in my life? Police are about as useless as an ashtray on a motorcycle.

"So that was that? Just a run-of-the-mill hold up? Your mother was in the wrong place at the wrong time?"

She nods, clearly having bought the police story hook, line, and sinker. Probably better that way. Why should she torment herself wondering about the truth?

Truth is a funny thing. Sure, Charleigh's mother was murdered in a hold up. Pawn shops get robbed because they have cash, jewelry, and usually, shitty, low-tech security. I guess even a dump like Gates's could be robbed.

And while what Charleigh believes may be the truth, or some version of it, something tells me that's not the end of the story. I'd bet my every last penny that Mrs. Gates was offed because of something her dumb fuck husband did. Once again, the asshole was in debt, or he did something to tick off the wrong person. So they took out his wife.

Harsh, yes. But I've seen it done before.

"How'd your dad take it?" I ask.

She looks at me, wide-eyed. "He never got over it.

Sank into this deep depression. My older sister had to take care of all of us. She still does, really, even though she lives in New York. Pops took down all photos and reminders of Mother, and we're not allowed to even mention her."

Mystery solved. It *was* his fault his wife took a bullet. That man has been eaten alive by guilt and the secret he's kept.

But again, I'll keep this piece of information to myself.

"So, that's when the youngest one lost her shit?"

Charleigh pulls her hair over her shoulder and starts making a long braid. I want to reach over and run my fingers through those long locks. But I don't.

"Yeah. Seems like it. Although who knows. Maybe she would have been a troubled kid even if my mom hadn't died."

How many murders are labelled random, which are anything but? Charleigh's mom, my parents... such bullshit.

"You're a good sister, Charleigh."

She shrugs and pulls an elastic band off her wrist to tie off her braid. "I try. Evie sort of... responds to me. At least more than anyone else."

"My brothers and I are tight. They really supported me... in the past."

She looks my way. "Did… something happen? Something bad?"

Well, fuck. I had to go and open my big goddamned mouth about the lowest period of my life.

"I… I lost my girlfriend a few years back. She was killed in a car wreck. I was driving and walked away without a scratch."

I look straight ahead, chafing at the thought of Charleigh pitying me. I can't have that. My hands grip the steering wheel so tightly my knuckles are white. Not one of my favorite topics, and yet I'm the dumbass who brought it up.

I force myself to stretch out my fingers, to get the blood circulating through them again.

Everyone says it wasn't my fault, but that's bullshit. It was my fault and I've suffered every day since. I will continue to. As I should.

"I'm sorry to hear that," Charleigh says. "Must have been awful."

Still is awful, truth be told. I hope it always will be. Best way to atone, if you ask me, is to let yourself suffer. Endlessly.

Turns out I'm a fucking champ at that.

I don't bother adding how Charleigh resembles her. It's time to change the subject.

I pull into the club parking lot and stop the car

but don't get out. Charleigh has her fingers ready to pull the door handle but doesn't move either, waiting for me.

It's almost as if she wants to spend more time together. Almost.

"Do you think your sister was wondering who I was today? In the principal's office?"

Charleigh nods slowly. "Yeah. I'm surprised she didn't come right out and ask. She's usually pretty straightforward that way. She must have been freaked out about getting in trouble."

Interesting, for a serial offender. I got in trouble a lot as a kid, and once you go down that rabbit hole, you don't give a shit about digging yourself in deeper. You get to a point where there's nothing left to lose.

Charleigh's about to say something more, but Vadik walks out of the club and heads for his car. When he sees the two of us, he frowns and changes direction.

Heading toward us.

"Time to go in," I say.

CHAPTER THIRTY-FIVE

KIR

"I told you not to get soft over her," Vadik says, getting in my face.

I knew the moment he saw us in the car, he'd get the wrong idea.

But is it the wrong idea? Maybe I am getting soft.

Which won't do. Not at all.

I adjust my necktie in preparation for the evening's events. My brothers and I occasionally invite certain high-roller club members to exclusive gatherings, especially since Uncle Mikey disappeared. We want them to know we're here for them, and that the club is going nowhere. They like the one-on-one time with us. It makes them feel special.

Normally, I don't look forward to these nights. But tonight is different.

Charleigh is serving. The thought of watching her work the room in her high heels and short skirt, delivering drinks and making small talk with our members, already has me semi-hard. In fact, I turn away from my brother so he can't see, not that he makes a habit of looking at my dick.

I don't want to risk it.

The way she handled her kid sister's principal today was masterful, composed, and understanding of the woman's position. Of course, it doesn't hurt that she's a stunner, with her statuesque figure and chestnut hair. In fact, she turned the heads of every person who walked by the office while we were in there. Charleigh has a lot to offer. An auction might not be the right way to go with her.

But I'll chance that conversation with my brothers another day. At the moment, it's showtime.

When we enter the lounge, members flock around us like we're goddamned rock stars. They really just want access, though—access to our businesses, girls, booze—you name it. I could get hit by a car tomorrow and none of them would give a shit.

But they'd probably show up at my funeral, just like they did my father's.

Vadik beams, nodding cordially at the men extending their hands for a shake, just like our father used to. As the oldest, he has some sort of compulsion to carry things on just the way Papa did. Niko and I don't really mind. Our father ran an excellent business and as hard as he tried, our loser uncle couldn't quite destroy it.

My suspicions about Charleigh's talents are not going unfounded. While there are a few girls serving the crowd tonight, beauties, all of them, none turn heads quite like our tall, lovely brunette. She bends to place drinks on the tables without showing her ass, smiles and chats with the men who make the effort, and doesn't spill a thing.

"I know what you're up to, you know."

Vadik. Again.

The members have all returned to their seats for the time being and the three of us are settling in at our own table. We'll start making rounds again, soon.

I sigh. "Get off my back. Seriously," I say, sucking back a large swig of scotch. "Christ, you're the one who had her panties down, coming all over your hand. Why don't you take a look at your own behavior? You should have seen your face."

He picks a piece of lint off his trousers as a distraction. That means he's pissed. He's never liked being called out. Not that anyone likes it. He just takes extra offense to it.

"Don't worry about me," he growls. "I've got my

shit under control. But you've got it all over for her. Get ahold of yourself."

Niko looks between the two of us, then around the room, trying to ignore us.

Now it's my turn to get in his face. "You know, Vadik," I say, lowering my voice, "you need to get over this big-brother-in-charge shit. It's getting old."

He looks around the room, grasping for patience. It's funny when you work with family. You know just how to push their buttons and read their every movement.

It's a blessing and a curse, as they say.

He turns back to me, but keeps his gaze locked on the drink in my hand, signifying I've really gotten under his skin. "You're so full of shit," he hisses. "This has nothing to do with being the oldest, Kir. It's about Papa's legacy. And our future. Don't blow it over some pussy."

CHAPTER THIRTY-SIX

CHARLEIGH

"How much do you think she'll bring in?" Vadik asks. "And she'd still better be a fucking virgin."

Are they talking about me? What do they mean by 'bring in?' Isn't serving drinks to their members payment enough for my father's debts? And why is my virginity, which is none of their damn business, such an obsession for them?

What more do they want from me? They've already taken everything.

Actually, it's obvious. I tremble as the reality of my situation gets increasingly more obvious. And horrific.

I consider inching closer to their table so I can hear more while the bartender loads me up with dry martinis for the drunks in the corner. But the flush washing over me from what I've already heard, the kind you feel before you faint or barf, tells me I've eavesdropped all I need to.

Get back to work and stop snooping.

You are just making things worse.

These men. They don't care about me, I have to keep reminding myself. Sure, they've given me nice accommodations and invited me to dine with them. And yes, Vadik has magical fingers, and Kir took me to resolve my sister's problem at school. Niko shared his story of how he is the result of his mother's affair, and I now know what happened to their parents.

Big fucking deal. Doesn't make us friends.

None of it means shit because all they really care about is making money off me.

These men are beasts, plain and simple. I hate them and I hate everything about them—their good looks, their arrogant confidence, their assuredness that they will always get what they want, no matter what they have to do for it.

I've been on my feet for three hours straight, not that any of the club members would know that. I quickly and pleasantly serve their cocktails, and chat when they want to know more about me or just discuss the weather. Back and forth, from the bar to the tables and back.

I'm not sure I've ever done anything more tedious.

And for nearly that whole time, amidst their socializing with members, Vadik, Kir, and Niko have scarcely taken their eyes off me.

If they think so little of me, why do they bother?

For the umpteenth time that shift, I pass their table, catching Niko's gaze. I don't want to look at them, but one quick glance and I'm caught.

A lock of blond hair hangs across his forehead like it often does, almost obscuring one of his eyes, like he's some sort of rakish pirate. In a split second, he smiles at me with an upturn of the corner of his mouth. My heart skips a beat.

Or three.

Dammit. Why does he—really, all the guys—have this effect on me? They're about to ruin my life, and all I can do is think about how sexy and seductive they are.

Bastards.

On my next trip past them, juggling a heavy tray of empty glasses, I keep my gaze straight ahead.

I will not look at them. I will not give them the satisfaction.

I will not associate or be friendly with anyone assessing my 'worth.'

And just when I let my tiny amount of self-righteousness offer me some comfort, two fingers pinch my ass so hard the glasses tumble off my tray, smashing into everyone and everything surrounding me.

CHAPTER THIRTY-SEVEN

CHARLEIGH

There is an uproar with people jumping to their feet, wiping off the alcohol I spilled on their suit jackets, but I am first and foremost concerned with getting back up. I'm sprawled on the soft carpet, fortunately, but when I push myself up, I scream from the pain in my left hand.

I recoil at what I see—a shard of glass sticking out of my palm, with blood pooling slowly around it, like something from a horror movie—which pretty much reflects the status of my life at the moment. Without thinking, I yank the piece of glass out. Big mistake. Not only have I now exponentially increased my pain but have also left an open hole in my hand, where the glass was temporarily plugging it.

My palm fills with a stream of pulsing blood.

Dominika is there in a second, pulling me up by my good arm and keeping her distance from the blood. "C'mon," she barks. "Get out of here with that mess. Look what you're doing, all over the carpet."

Before my mouth can even drop open, and before the urge to smack her ugly face makes me do something to endanger my life more than it already is, the bartender is there with a couple towels. Niko grabs them from him. He wraps one around my hand, so tight it almost hurts, and lifts my arm above my head.

"Sit here," he demands.

Dominika scowls at having been overruled.

I sit with my hand up in the air, and before I can even blink, Niko has pulled some man I've never seen out of his seat and is shaking him by the lapels.

"You fuck," he growls. "Get out of here. And never come back."

The man, balding and pockmarked, holds his hands up in surrender. "Easy there, guy," he pleads, shocked that his behavior's considered out of line. "I was just having a little fun with the help."

He looks back at his buddies, who have also gotten to their feet. But they aren't paying any attention to him.

They are focused on the Alekseev brothers, waiting to see if they are in line for the same treatment as their imprudent friend.

With no backup, the man takes a few steps, glancing toward the lounge exit. He's clearly gotten the message he's never coming back, but he also seems worried about making it out alive.

His concerns are not unfounded. In the next moment, the fury in Niko's eyes turns into a closed fist in the center of the man's face.

He stumbles back, blood flowing out of his nostrils like a garden hose, and into his friends who no longer want anything to do with him. One of them grabs him from under the arms, and drags him out, the door slamming behind them.

His other friends respond with a chorus of *I'm sorry, That guy's an asshole, Let us pay for this mess,* and *Are you okay, Miss?*

Niko shakes out the hand he hit the man with, opening and closing his fingers, and turns back to me. "Let me see your hand, Charleigh. You might need stitches."

Not so fast.

He might have come to my defense, but I'm not giving him the pleasure of ensuring his 'investment' remains flawless. I push to my feet with my good hand, ignoring the wooziness that's making the room spin, and run past all of them, including Dominika. I head to my room, making sure to drip blood all the way down the hallway. I hope it stains. I want them to remember me when I'm gone.

CHAPTER THIRTY-EIGHT

By the time my hand stops bleeding, every last towel in my room is dotted with blood, probably ruined, and I couldn't give a shit. Not only are the towels stained with red, so is my bedspread, the floor, and the bathroom sink and tub where I attempted to clean up

Fuck this place and the beastly brothers who own it. I plan to ruin as much as I can in the time that I'm here.

They have no regard for me or my little sister, and certainly not my father, forcing me to repay his debts and threatening to add Evie to their 'collection.'

I don't care if I signed their freaking contract. I had no choice. That's not what I call 'voluntary.'

They can kiss my ass.

"Hello?" someone calls from my doorway.

I look over and see Niko peering in. Dammit, that door needs a lock.

But I sit up in bed anyway, turning off the Spotify station I was about to start streaming to forget my life for a moment. "Hi," I say.

I find myself smoothing my hair and straightening out my T-shirt.

So much for my tough guy act.

He stands across the room, arms crossed. Almost like he isn't sure whether or not he should come in.

Funny time to be all bashful, when you've just been talking about making money off me.

The day I walked out the door to get Evie at school, it was so easy to leave. Granted, I wasn't even really trying to sneak out. I honestly intended to come back as soon as I got her principal settled down. But if it were so easy in broad daylight to just leave, why not give it a try in the dead of night, when the club is relatively quiet, the guys are asleep, and security is on the lax side?

I look back at Niko, crossing the room toward me, rubbing his hand along the side of his neck like he's had a long day or something, and my resolve crumbles.

I hate that. I goddamn hate it.

"Looks like you slaughtered someone in here," he says, looking around.

I momentarily worry he's going to be pissed at the mess. But then I remember I don't care.

Not much, anyway.

I shrug it off. "Yeah, well, that's what happens when a creep pinches your ass and you fall and cut yourself on broken glass."

I hold my hand up, wrapped in the last clean towel I have. The blood on the outside of it is beginning to dry to a crackly brown, which tells me it's no longer flowing from my wound. That's a good sign. At least I won't need stitches.

"Your hand feeling better?" he asks, taking a seat on the edge of my bed.

Just make yourself at home, buddy.

I remind myself to be polite and throw him a shy half-smile.

He begins to tell me how the guy they kicked out is banned for life, etcetera, etcetera, as if I give a shit they are so valiantly defending my honor, and my thoughts wander back to escaping. But that would just leave Pops and Evie worse off than they already are.

The only other option is to stick around and see what the guys have planned for me. Although I'm pretty sure I have an idea.

Or... find some way to escalate the tension between the brothers and Dimitri so they all destroy each other. Could I actually do that? Pit them against each other so they fight to the death?

That would be some first class-level cunning shit.

As I'm weighing my options, Niko takes my hand, the one in the big, bloodied towel, and slowly unwraps it. "Hey. It's looking good. Stopped bleeding. But look, you have to be careful not to open this up again."

He pulls a roll of gauze out of his pocket. "C'mon. Let's wash this off and then I'll wrap it."

"Guess you were a Boy Scout, huh?"

He laughs as he places my hand under a gentle stream of cold water. It stings like hell. "Not exactly a Boy Scout. But I do know some first aid. Comes in handy in my line of work—"

He cuts himself off, gently rubbing the dried blood from my hand with his thumb. Even after the blood is pretty much gone, he keeps rubbing like he's mesmerized. When I clear my throat, he snaps to, dabbing my hand with a clean corner of a bloody towel. After, he wraps the gauze around it, sure to build up several protective layers where the cut is.

Still holding my now-clean and bandaged hand, he surprises me by lifting it to his lips and kissing one of my fingers. Then, moving along, he kisses each, one by one, until he reaches my thumb.

His touch is so damned nice, I'm unable to do the one thing I know I should—grab my hand out of his and suggest he fuck right off. I imagine telling him to get out of my room and leave me the hell alone, but the words never pass my lips.

Instead, my eyes flutter closed. I don't say I hate him and his brothers, their stupid club, their sleazy patrons, and that they got my dad hooked on gambling and let him pile up so much debt that I'm saddled with paying it off. That whatever they do with me will result in bad news for Evie, because I'm the only person in the world who gives a shit about her.

I don't tell him the harm they are causing my family is so far out of proportion to what my father owes, it's ridiculous, and that their desire to 'save face' and be the 'big guys' makes them nothing more than a bunch of assholes—not the alpha men they want the world to know they are.

Do I share any of this with him?

Hell no. Apparently, I'm just as much an asshole as the Alekseevs are, because while my eyes have been closed, while Niko kisses my fingertips, he takes a step closer, and kisses my lips.

And yes, I am kissing him right back.

CHAPTER THIRTY-NINE

CHARLEIGH

There's no stopping. I mean, I obviously know I should. But this is one of those times in life where logic serves no purpose. Responsibility? Right out the window. Good judgment?

Like it's never existed, not for one day in my pathetic life.

Right now, an absolutely beautiful man is running a finger along my chin, brushing his lips over mine, and that's all I care about. The rest of the world can disintegrate around me, and I won't give a shit because I not only got this man's attention but also got him to kiss me.

So fuck off, universe.

He pulls back for a moment, and I open my eyes.

Without a word, he surprises me again with the presumptuous act of unbuckling his belt and opening his trousers. Reaching through a tangle of shirt tails, he pulls out his erection, hard and veiny, with a bulbous, purple tip.

Do I tell him to go to hell? That I'm not his whore?

'Course not.

He places a hand on my shoulder and with gentle pressure, lets me know what he wants.

And I'm so here for it.

God forgive me.

I grab one of the dirty towels and pile it under my knees to protect them from the hard bathroom floor tiles. I look at Niko right there, right in front of my face, and recall the couple other times—I think I was still in high school—when I sucked a guy's hard-on. It was okay, not horrible, but I have never been eager to do it again.

Not that I had the chance. The one pseudo-boyfriend I had for less than a month was scared off. Apparently, he didn't want to tell his parents he was dating a girl whose dad owned a pawn shop. It wasn't respectable enough for them. I didn't bother with guys after that. Too much trouble.

But this is different. I don't know why, but it is.

I want Niko in my mouth so I can pleasure him like I see on the porn sites I watch on my phone when I touch myself at night. I want to hear him moan, breathe hard, and call my name when he explodes.

Any shyness or hesitation that might have plagued me in real life—before the Alekseevs—is nonexistent.

"Go ahead. Take it, pretty girl," he says quietly.

A shiver of anticipation darts down my spine as I look up at him and he smiles back, like I'm good and obedient. I love it.

I wrap my hand around his girth, so fat my fingers don't meet, and lean forward to taste the drop of clear liquid on his tip.

"Mmmm," I moan, surprising myself as much as him.

"Beautiful baby likes it, huh?"

Looking up at him, I nod. Goddamn, he's so handsome with his tousled blond hair and facial scruff that I'm out of my mind with the headiness of my longing.

"I like it. I do," I whisper as if I don't want anyone to hear me say it.

He strokes a finger under my chin. "Such a pretty, pretty girl. Now open up that lovely mouth."

As if mesmerized by his praise, I part my lips to allow his cockhead to settle between my lips. I accept him, the large, smooth head and ridge that is the beginning of his shaft. With a deep breath, I take more of him.

But apparently, not enough.

CHAPTER FORTY

CHARLEIGH

"C'mon now," he says in a gruff tone I don't recognize, "I'm not teaching you to suck cock, baby. Either you do it well, or someone will have to teach you who's not nearly as nice as I am."

I freeze and look up, finding his eyes narrowed to dark slits. Is this really Niko? I squeeze my eyes shut as if I could block out his nasty words, until he growls at me again.

Is this what happens to men? You give them a little pleasure and they start demanding more? Like hungry beasts?

Fine. If that's what he wants, that's what he'll get. And if he wants to choke me with his giant erection, maybe that's just as well too.

Maybe he'll choke me to death. Put me out of my misery.

I take him deeper, deeper than I thought I could, and in contrast to his sharp words, he rocks his hips slightly, gently pulsing and sliding in and out of my mouth. In seconds, his scary tone is forgotten and I'm savoring him, wanting nothing more in the world at that moment than to make him feel good.

Because this is power.

I might not have much over my situation. Actually, I have *no* power over my situation. But I do have power over this moment. Men are ruled by their cocks, their need to come and spread their seed, and they'll often stop at nothing for the opportunity.

I will make this work for me. I will make Niko love me, if only for the time he's in my mouth. I will give him something unforgettable that he will come back to me again and again for.

He will become addicted to me, and while what I have to offer him is modest, he won't be able to live without it.

With a vigor I didn't know I possessed, I take him deeper, until he bangs the back of my throat and gags me. My eyes water, turning my mascara into soupy rivers, and saliva leaks out of the sides of my mouth and down my chin.

I wipe both away so as not to ruin the moment.

He lifts my chin so I can continue sucking him while our gazes are locked, a vulnerable position if ever there was one. We rock together and I feel his orgasm building like it's my own. He's getting close to exploding and it's all because of me.

He growls so loudly it echoes against the bathroom tile, and when he erupts down my throat, I choke for a moment, swallowing what I can, just like in the porn movies.

Through it, Niko keeps his eyes open and locked with mine, but the rest of his face distorts, first, as if he's angry, then as if he's in pain, and finally his mouth moves from a grimace to a roar that hits me like a prize, especially when it turns into a smile, one so big it thumps my heart.

Just as he pulls out and I'm catching my breath, my bedroom door flies open. I'm in full view, on my knees in front of Niko's still-hard cock, mopping up the small amount of semen that didn't make it down my throat and instead ended up on my chin and chest.

"Holy fuck. Guess your hand isn't bothering you too much," Kir booms, smiling ear to ear.

For a moment I want to roll into a little ball of disgrace, having been caught doing something so naughty, so animalistic.

So fun.

This is for pure pleasure. The man's pleasure.

And mine, no doubt about it.

I smile broadly, proud of myself and my prowess. I'm not ashamed. Not one bit. Why should I be?

"If it isn't my older brother. One of them anyway," Niko laughs, making no attempt to tuck himself back in his pants.

He takes my good hand and helps me back to my feet. I wobble for a moment as the circulation returns to my legs and reach for a clean towel for him. Then I remember there are none, thanks to my injured hand.

Oh well.

Kir approaches us and slaps Niko on the back and rubs a smudge of something off my face. "God, you two are cute together," he says.

My heart thumps. He's just kidding, of course, but what if we *were* 'together?' What if I were with any of these guys? They're so good-looking, with power and confidence to spare oozing from every pore. They're soulless men who make decisions that leave people devastated, but if I were with them, any of them, they'd protect me from the world's evils. I'd never have to be afraid again.

They would help me. And I would help them back.

Wouldn't someone like me—pleasant, thoughtful,

morally upright—bring the perfect balance to their lives?

Good god. How I've gone off the deep end.

"Hi Kir," I say, tilting my head flirtatiously. Might as well give it a shot. "We were just—"

He cuts me off. "Darlin', you don't have to explain yourself to me. But you have given me an idea."

Oh god.

"What would you say, beautiful, to coming over here to the bed with me?"

He runs his fingers through what are now tangles in my hair, and while it pulls, it also feels good. Heavenly, even.

"C'mon, baby," he says with a crook of his finger.

I follow him like my legs have a mind of their own. Any doubts I have fly out the window as I put one foot in front of the other like some sort of horny, mindless robot. I need to make him feel good just like I did Niko. I need to make him need me, too.

He loosens his tie and the tickle in my core intensifies. "Lie down, beautiful. And watch out for that hand. No more injuries for one day, okay?"

Hand? I forgot about my hand. I certainly forgot about my circumstances, that they aren't looking too bright. And if I can float in that timeless, blissful state of no pain or worries for a little longer, then I'm in.

CHAPTER FORTY-ONE

Niko

As soon as Kir shimmies Charleigh's sweatpants down her hips and a I get a look at her beautiful, bare pussy, I am hard again so fast it hurts.

It's a good hurt. The kind of hurt I like. And want more of.

I just exploded down this woman's throat and now I'm hard again, like a goddamned horny teenage boy.

What this woman does to me. Her quiet dignity and the red-hot passion lurking just below the surface of her propriety is the stuff of dreams.

Mine, anyway.

Sure, some guys like the kind of women who wouldn't know subtlety if it smacked them in the face. Not me. Understated women are something special. They are mysterious. They hold surprises. They don't tell you everything the first time you meet them. You've got to work for it.

I stand back and spot Kir's jacket and tie on the floor in the same pile where the rest of Charleigh's clothes are. He's running kisses up the inside of one thigh and down the other, leaving her writhing like she's possessed by the devil. Her slight smile is sweet and delicious and for a dangerous moment I imagine she's mine. As if she were here at the club as a permanent fixture. One where she was at my side. All the time.

Not being used to pay off her father's debts.

She catches me staring and settles a bit, pulling a pillow under her head and then extending a hand. While Kir is nibbling her inner thighs, I cross the room in hurried strides and bend to kiss her.

I can't help it. I wanted to taste her lips since the night we brought her back here, and now that I have, I want to again.

We guys, my brothers and I, should not be playing around with her. We have plans for the girl and need to keep her fresh and innocent. But damn if I can control myself when I'm around her. It's all I can do to keep my hands to myself.

My brothers are no different.

I am pretty damn sure they feel the same way, Vadik's warnings notwithstanding.

While something in the back of my mind is telling me to get the hell out of here, the taste of her lips on mine is just too good, too sweet to walk away from. Hell, if she were tainted with deadly poison, I wouldn't be able to stop myself.

"So beautiful, such a beautiful girl," I murmur, running a hand down to her breasts to find her nipples stiff from our attentions.

And damn if my own dick isn't begging for more, again, like a greedy little bastard, hanging out of my pants as it is.

In fact, fuck all these clothes. I leave Charleigh's lips and undress. I am the tidy one among my brothers, and lay my jacket and tie over a chair, followed by my dress shirt and the rest of my clothes, and last but not least, my boxers. If Kir weren't so busy between Charleigh's thighs, he'd poke fun at me. Not that I care.

And while I do this, my gaze never leaves her. She won't be around the club for long, so I know to enjoy her while I can.

"Niko, check this out," Kir says.

I stand next to where he's kneeling on the bed between Charleigh's legs. The bastard has her pussy spread open, all pink and juicy, and he's running her clit between the knuckles of his first and middle fingers.

"Careful there, brother," I warn.

She might be a delectable treat, but the best of her is reserved for whatever club member is willing to pay the most for her.

And her virginity.

CHAPTER FORTY-TWO

"Don't worry, Nik," Kir says. "Come see this clit."

I watch Charleigh's pussy respond. I saw it the other day when Vadik was playing with her, but it was from the other side of the dining table, and I had to get the fuck out of there for some privacy to jerk myself to relief.

But close up it's like seeing the Mona Lisa in the Louvre instead of in a stupid art history book.

Sublime perfection. A gift from God. If I believed in God.

And as my brother kneads and pulls her pink button, Charleigh writhes harder beneath him.

"We gotta get this clit pierced," Kir says. "What do you think?"

Before I can answer, Charleigh lifts her head from the pillow. "What?" she cries.

"Honey," Kir says, waving away her concern. "It's no big deal. Women do it all the time."

"Does it hurt?" she asks, dropping her head back on her pillow as Kir strokes her with his tongue.

"It hurts, baby. Of course it does. But it's not horrible from what I've been told. Besides, pain is good, isn't it?" I ask, taking a seat on the bed next to her and stroking my aching dick.

Talk about pain.

"Mmmm, so good," Kir whispers from between her legs.

"With a piercing, your pussy will be even more beautiful than it already is," I say, coming up with an idea. "Kir. Let's get our pretty girl on her hands and knees."

My brother pulls his face from between Charleigh's legs and smiles. "Here we go, baby," he says, flipping her over.

Charleigh climbs to her knees, looking around to see what happens next. And like we've done a dozen times before, because we *have*, my brother positions himself at her head, where he lays back with his hard-on nearly poking her in the eye. I get underneath her with my legs dangling off the bed and pull her sweet pussy right down onto my face as she straddles me.

Charleigh shrieks in surprise and then laughs. Her noise quickly quiets down because I am sure she now has a mouthful of my brother's cock, and the only sound she can make is licking and slurping.

And hearing her do exactly that makes me want to blow my wad again.

While on my back, I wrap an arm around Charleigh's ass and pull her so close and tight I'm almost suffocated by her sweet pussy. With my free hand, I stroke my dick hard, squeezing, releasing, and stroking to hold my cum as long as I can.

I know it won't be long, though.

I want more than anything to drive a couple fingers into her cunt, but I can't risk upsetting her virginity.

As much as I'd like to.

So I focus on sucking her clit and making little circles around her asshole until the very tip of my finger pops inside.

Our pretty girl goes wild, wagging her hips like a dog in heat, asking for—no, demanding—more. But I don't give it to her.

I want to leave her wanting. Needy. Coming back for more.

And from the sounds of my brother, she's now fully focused on him and not her bottom. I can't see from my vantage point but the way she's nearly being thrown off the bed—shit, even I have to hang on at this point—I know Kir is about to empty his load into her mouth.

As soon as he's done roaring like a maniac, I return my focus to Charleigh's clit. In moments, she's convulsing above me, grinding into my face and taking my breath away. With one last gasp, she shudders with a shriek.

Fuck yeah. That's our girl.

CHAPTER FORTY-THREE

"You missed all the fun, loser."

Vadik looks up from his desk. "What? You beat the shit out of the guy who grabbed Charleigh?"

Kir and I look at each other.

"Well, that's a given, Vad. The guys downstairs took care of that, though."

He frowns at us both, irritated we interrupted his work. Fucker needs to take a goddamn chill pill. "Then how did your clothes get so messed up?" he asks, gesturing with his chin.

I look down at myself, then at Kir. Yeah, we're a wrinkled, rumpled mess. But we're also smiling like lunatics.

Do I really look like I just beat the shit out of

someone, rather than coming in some hot girl's mouth?

"*Really?*" he asks when he puts it all together.

My brother's a regular Einstein, he is.

"Look, you assholes, you need some control when it comes to Charleigh. Don't be like the loser who grabbed her."

I roll my eyes. Can't help it. "If I remember correctly, it's you who put on a show with her the other night. Vad, you opened Pandora's Box. And now we're all fucked."

He looks down at his desk, shaking his head.

"You've got the hots for her, huh?" he asks, getting to his feet and closing in on me.

I shrug. "Who doesn't? Show me one man who can resist her. Yourself included."

He steps closer to me, his usual intimidation tactic. But he forgets we're not kids anymore. What once worked to keep me in my place expired years ago, no matter how often he tries.

"Probably just as well you didn't happen by, Vad," Kir says. "I'd say she's scared to death of your mean ass."

Big brother doesn't like being mocked.

Vadik's lower jaw shifts, and I know he's grinding his teeth. Hard. He's been doing more of that, lately.

"Hey, we talked about piercing her clit. What do you think?" I ask, egging him on.

He presses his lips together, grabs the glass full of vodka off his desk, and flings it across the room, where it crashes and splatters on the dark wood wall.

Someone's going to have fun cleaning that mess up.

A knock sounds on Vadik's office door, bringing the tension in the room down a notch. Dominika joins us, and the tension ramps right back up.

Of course.

It's not that we don't like her, exactly. She works hard for the club and has been a loyal employee since my dad brought her on when we were kids.

But there is no doubt she is… difficult. In fact, sometimes she's such a pain in the ass I wonder how long my brothers and I will keep her on. I know Papa would want us to make sure she's taken care of. He had his… reasons for that.

We don't have the same obligation.

"Dominika," I say by way of greeting. Most people, I might ask how they are or how their day has been.

With Dominika, there are no such pleasantries. And even if there were, I wouldn't care whether she was having a good day or not.

It's hard to see the woman who was your father's mistress for the better part of twenty years in an objective light.

She gets right to the point. "We're set for next weekend's auction for Charleigh. We didn't have much time, but I've wrangled the highest of our high-roller members. They're coming in from all over the world and a few will attend virtually over Zoom."

I don't know whether to hug her or tell her to get the fuck out.

The reality of what my brothers and I are about to do hits me. Men—a lot of men—are going to see the same thing I do in Charleigh, and they are going to want her just as much as I do. Maybe more. And they are going to spend money for the privilege. A lot of it.

Something about that leaves a sour taste in my mouth. But I say nothing. It's not the right time. First, Dominika doesn't need to know anything that might be perceived as a weakness when it comes to my brothers and me, and second, I want to make sure Vadik and Kir are ready to hear my thoughts when I express them. Right now, I'm afraid they are not.

They are seeing dollar signs, and there's little my brothers like more than money.

"Thank you, Dominika," Vadik says. "I know we didn't give you much time to pull this together. There will be a nice bonus in it for you, for gathering our big spenders."

At the mention of money, Dominika's heavily-painted face brightens. "I'm happy to do it. I'm assuming Charleigh doesn't know yet? It will be very… entertaining to see her when she learns of her fate."

Dominika grins, her smoke-stained teeth so rancid I have to look away, and all I can think is how she looks like a witch that eats babies, that's how cruel and hateful she is.

I mean, my brothers and I are surely no saints. But we also do not get gratuitous pleasure in seeing others suffer.

As soon as she's gone, the closed door not completely eliminating her cheap perfume, I turn to my brothers. "You know what? I hate that cunt. When are we getting rid of her?"

If we've had this conversation once, we've had it a hundred times. And Vadik gives his usual answer, with Kir nodding his approval.

"C'mon now, Niko, you know we need her for continuity. At least until the club is on more solid ground. Once we've accomplished that, we'll talk again. But right now, she's going nowhere."

He is right. We do need her. Which makes me resent her even more.

We're sending Charleigh away and keeping Dominika around.

Something about that is goddamn backwards.

CHAPTER FORTY-FOUR

"Someone's got to tell her. Charleigh deserves to know what's in store for her," I say.

Kir grabs the chair opposite Vadik's desk and leans back with a stretch. I know he's trying to act all casual and shit, but he's got to be thinking along the same lines as me.

Jesus, the girl deserves to know she's about to be auctioned to some fucker who wants to buy her virginity. My fists clench at the thought, so I stuff them in my trouser pockets.

It's a business transaction, I remind myself. That's all it is.

"Do you think she really has no idea? I mean, is she that clueless?" Vadik asks. "Eh, let Dominika tell her. She's her problem, anyway."

Goddamn, sometimes I want to smack him.

"I want to tell her before Dominika does. The woman will get too much pleasure out of freaking her out."

I can see it now, Dominika laughing and telling Charleigh to just suck it up.

"Who do you think will bid on her? I mean, like really bid? Like big fucking bucks?" Kir asks. "She could go for a lot. I mean, I wouldn't mind popping that cherry. She sucks dick like a champ. I can only imagine—"

"*Stop*," I holler, surprising myself.

And pissing myself off too. Just gave myself away, dammit.

Kir doesn't miss a beat. "Look, little bro, I like her too. She's sweet as honey. But she's not ours. You need to keep that in mind."

I glare at him.

"Unless…" he continues, "*you* want to buy her."

The room is quiet for a moment.

"Out of the question," Vadik says, getting to his feet. "You don't have the kind of money we can raise from our members. Not many people do. Now c'mon. We've got work to do. All of us."

"I hear Alexei is due for a visit," Kir says as he joins Vadik in standing. "That old fucker," he chuckles.

Holy Christ. This is not good news.

Alexei is old school. Old, and old school. He came over from Russia before my father did, and helped him with some business dealings. He thinks the Alekseev family is still indebted to him and acts like a VIP around the club because he was friends with Papa. We don't let him think otherwise, but the day he finally keels over and dies will be a happy one for us.

When he finds out about Charleigh, he's going to want her for himself. He can afford to pay for her. He's the richest billionaire in our faction.

I mean, my brothers and I have money. But this man has *serious* fucking money. Like he can buy anything he wants anytime, kind of money. A jet, a yacht, an island.

A beautiful young virgin coveted by many.

Shit, he might even bid her up to show the rest of the *slobs*, as he calls them, just how rich he is. Gain their envy. In his way of thinking, envy equals respect.

Whoever has the most toys—or anything of value, really—wins. Alexei likes to win. And he usually does.

Vadik takes a deep breath and looks between my brother and me. He knows something. Something he doesn't want to tell us.

Or something he doesn't want to tell *me*.

"I... got news for you, guys," he says.

God fucking dammit. I knew Alexei was going to get wind of this Charleigh shit. I can't let him have her, no matter how much he pays. I won't.

Rumor has it that the last virgin he 'acquired' ended up in the hospital from his rough treatment and later found out she's no longer able to have children.

I've always wondered if that were true. I mean, while the *Pakhan* tries to stomp out gossip and shit, a story that outrageous will always make its way through the pipeline, regardless.

"What, Vadik? What do you mean, *news*?" I ask.

Stay cool. Stay cool.

"Seems Dominika told him all about her. Sent him photos and everything. And he's made a preemptive bid."

CHAPTER FORTY-FIVE

Charleigh

I serve a bottle of wine that probably cost more than my dad's pawn shop makes in a year, and head back to the bar for something to lean on, just for a moment. The lounge isn't too busy yet—it's that in-between time where the day drinkers are leaving and the happy hour crowd has yet to arrive. When those folks are done, usually sometime in the early evening, probably to rush home to wives and children, they're replaced by men who don't leave until all hours of the morning.

These are the die-hards. When you waitress on this shift, you can count on running the entire time. No breaks, not even to go to the bathroom. But I'm not complaining. Although we're not supposed to accept them, these guys tip, and very generously. So,

I made a little hole in my mattress where I'm hiding my cash. I need to make sure it gets to Evie somehow.

Probably not the best idea to entrust a couple thousand dollars to a kid, but I can't keep it with me and I'm sure as hell not giving it to my father. I'll ask her to put it aside for the two of us. Who knows whether she'll honor my request or totally blow it off. She's been so volatile in the last year. Actually, she's pretty much always been volatile, but in the last year it's gotten worse. Fights and all that. Things I never did.

Which makes it difficult to understand why she does them.

I don't give her a hard time. There are enough other people around her who take care of that. I just try to support her and keep reminding her I know she'll do great things. When she's ready.

Because the lounge is slow right now, I reach behind the bar for my water bottle and take a swig. Unfortunately, I'm not even finished before Dominika descends on me.

Most of the time she stays out of the lounge, dealing with other parts of the club, but the strippers don't go on until later, so I guess she has nothing else to do but give me a hard time.

Such a godawful woman.

"Get off the bar. Now."

I lift my elbow off the bar and stand at attention. I'm not exactly sure that's what she wants, but I don't know what else to do.

She takes a step closer, and the bartender in the background shakes his head like he's seen this before. "Don't let me catch you like that again."

It would be so satisfying to pour a drink over her head and watch all that makeup slither off her face.

"No problem, Dominika," I say, faking remorse by looking down at my feet. "Won't happen again."

Satisfied by my atonement, she surveys the room and her face lights up when she sees the expensive bottle of wine our only occupied table is enjoying.

"Say, Dominika, I haven't seen Stacey in a while. Where has she been?" I ask.

Now that I think of it, I haven't seen Stacey since the day she started to tell me something about the club, something that seemed confidential, when we were interrupted by Dominika. It's odd she hasn't been around. I thought she took a lot of shifts because the money was so good. Maybe she's on vacation?

Do strippers take vacations?

Dominika crosses her arms and sneers at me. Of course. Would it kill her to give me a normal, respectable, straight answer? "Don't worry about where Stacey is. People come and go here all the time. You may see them once or twice, and then they're gone. Don't bother making friends with anyone. They won't do you any good, and will turn on you the first time they need something."

She scoffs, satisfied with having shared her ugly perspective.

I've never hated anyone in my life. But I do now.

"I thought Stacey worked here for a long time. As a stripper. Right?"

She was so kind to me. What could have happened to her?

Dominika rolls her eyes. "Like I told you, people cycle in and out of this place. You'll learn that. In fact, you won't be here long, either. But you probably already know that, don't you? The Alekseev brothers have told you, yes?"

CHAPTER FORTY-SIX

CHARLEIGH

Something grinds in my stomach and I want to steady myself on the bar. But I dare not touch it again. "Um, no, they haven't told me anything specific. I've been wondering how long I need to stay here to fulfill my father's obligation. Am I already that close to being finished?"

Please say yes, please say yes. I can get back to my course. I've missed some classroom time and one exam, but I can make it up. I know I can. And Luci will help me.

But Dominika just laughs, spewing her rank breath. "Honey, you have no fucking clue, do you?"

Clue about what?

I shake my head slowly, my mouth suddenly too dry to speak.

Do I really want to hear this? Or would it be better to remain in the dark?

"Christ, I don't know what they're saving the exciting news for." She looks around like she's going to tell me something she shouldn't. I brace myself. "You're to be auctioned to pay your father's debts. You thought cocktailing a few hours in a short skirt and high heels would absolve his obligations? Are you fucking kidding me?"

I'm about to ask her to repeat herself because what she's saying is so outrageous that I'm sure I heard her wrong. I must have. But no, when I think about it for a moment, I heard her loud and clear.

If I had a sharp object, I'd stab her in the neck.

She's full of shit and trying to scare me. That's how awful she is. Empty, void of what makes someone human, missing everything that separates us from other animals.

Babbling on about something, I watch her lips move. But I hear nothing. I can say nothing.

I finally get my voice back and interrupt. "Wait. Wh… what do you mean, *auctioned*?"

She smiles and I want to wipe the smug off her hideous face. She's having fun. Way too much fun.

She's got me and she knows it.

She slams her hands on her hips. "You really are that stupid," she scolds. "An auction is where something is sold to the highest bidder. And that some-thing being sold, in this case, is you and your virginity."

This is the deal? *This* is their payment?

Does my father know this?

Does everyone, including Stacey from the dressing room know this? Except me?

I grab the edge of the bar for balance. I don't care if it pisses off Dominika or not. I figure it will piss her off a lot more if I pass out in view of members.

Her words tumble around in my mind, frag-mented and out of order.

Auction.

Me.

And my virginity.

For sale.

Because my father got himself into debt, so much that he could only pay it off by pimping me out.

I can't… I won't…

My mother would be ashamed. So ashamed.

"Oh, I meant to add, Charleigh," Dominika continues, ignoring the fact that I'm swaying right in front of her, "there's someone very special coming to meet you this evening, someone who I think will be very interested in you. In fact, I suspect he'll be along… right about now."

As if on cue, because of course, the lounge door

opens. Two tall, buff men in tailored suits enter, scanning the room like they're looking for someone. They nod at each other and turn to usher a third person through the door.

A trollish old man totters in, and each of the guys takes one of his sides, looking in part ready to take orders from him, and in part ready to prop him up should he fall over.

Who the hell is this?

He myopically heads toward Dominika, probably attracted to her beacon of fiery red hair, when his gaze shifts to me.

And as if no one else is in the room, heads straight my way.

CHAPTER FORTY-SEVEN

CHARLEIGH

I'm reeling from the bombshell news Dominika so gleefully dumped on me, her eyes literally glittering as she did, like she was informing me I won the lottery or something. That's how excited she was to lay her horror on me, and I think she even stood a little taller when she did, so pleased she was with herself.

I have no doubt she would have been that much more happy had I fallen to my knees and begged for mercy, shedding tears all over her stilettos.

And as if the news that I am going to be *auctioned* like a human piece of cattle isn't horrifying enough, a troll of a man who acts like he walks on water seems to have taken a liking to me.

As if the deal is done. The sale is made and the buyer is awaiting delivery.

My thoughts ricochet back and forth between this man, who seems only to use a first name—Alexei—and the betrayal I feel on the part of the brothers. Haven't our intimate moments meant anything? Didn't they look in my eyes as they came?

What about my *power*?

The power I stupidly thought I held over them…

Any my plan to pit them against Dimitri, to the point of mutual destruction.

What is wrong with these people?

And Alexei. Seriously, how did such an unappealing specimen of sub-humanity come into the sort of power where people all but bow and kiss his feet when he enters a room?

Truly. When he arrived, the few club members in attendance, enjoying their lovely wine, stopped talking. They looked at each other briefly with expressions I didn't understand, then jumped to their feet and smiled in his direction.

I observe all this in a brief moment because after that, I have to focus on the creature before me, whose rheumy eyes look me over like I am a tasty meal.

By contrast, and not for the first time today, it's all I can do not to vomit.

Alexei's complexion—I shudder every time I think his name—is an unhealthy yellow-gray. His puffy face is dotted with protruding moles, and what little hair he has is combed over his head, held in place with some sort of greasy substance.

I know this because he's of a height where, in my heels, I look down on the top of his head.

His smoke-tinged voice drips with carnality, and when he runs a smoke-stained finger along my bare bicep, I involuntarily recoil.

It's like being touched by a piece of rotten garbage. And he probably has no freaking idea I feel this way about his repulsive ass.

Naturally, Dominika's right there, shoving me toward him.

"Charleigh," he croons. "I've heard so much about you." His tone is flat but oily and runs down my skin, leaving a smelly, sticky residue I want to scratch until I bleed.

Once again, my stomach flips, like some sort of warning bell.

I glance at Dominika who is, of course, beaming. She's behind all this. It's clear as day.

How a grotesque man like this generates the reaction he does in those around him—Dominika's fawning and the attention of the club members—is beyond me. But when I think about it further, I guess it's not. I'm learning about this world, and its strange idiosyncrasies.

Money is all you need.

And the more you have, the better. Nothing else matters. That's the rule here, where power and respect are bought rather than earned.

"Who is that gross man? And why won't he leave me alone?" I ask Niko later. I'm torn between relief at seeing a familiar face, and the temptation to stab him in the heart for wanting to sell me at auction.

Niko's looking at me, but isn't really focused, and clearly does not see the pleading in my eyes. The question is, can he do anything to help?

Will he do anything to help?

Please, please let this be a nightmare I wake from. Maybe I should have been a praying person, one of devout faith like my mother.

A lot of good that did her.

No amount of praying is going to release me from this, not that God wants to hear what I have to say anyway.

And thank goodness Mother isn't around to see what's become of our family. If she were still here, this would surely kill her.

I thought Niko might provide some hope, and if not some hope, some insights. But when I see his reaction, or lack thereof, I'm not so sure.

He looks around the lounge like he's searching for something. "I'll remind him of the rules," he says distractedly. "I... I have some things to take care of today."

He finally looks at me, and there's something different about him, something I've not seen before. He's dark and cold. Hard. His lips twitch, I'm pretty sure involuntarily.

"Niko? What's going on?" I ask.

Across the room, the bartender is waving at me to come pick up the drinks he's poured. I throw him a pleading look, not at all certain he can read it, but I am desperate for a few more moments with Niko.

He rubs his chin, then scrapes his hair back and off his forehead. "We just got word that a shipment containing important cargo is missing. I... I don't have time for anything else right now."

I see a flash of regret in his eyes, or maybe I *want* to see it so badly, I am imagining it. But his brusqueness really says it all. He has priorities and for me to think I might be one of them is naïve and stupid.

"What kind of cargo, Niko?"

"Guns," he says simply. "I have to go."

I watch him retreat. What had he been looking for in the lounge? It's nearly empty, aside from the men drinking expensive wine, and the troll Alexei, being fawned over by Dominika, and watched over by the men who I finally figured out are his bodyguards.

I want to believe Niko stopped by to check on me. True, he has no time for me right now. He's got to take care of business.

But we have a connection. Right?

Yeah, a connection to an auction.

I shudder to think that, on top of the things carried out in the club, the guys also have business dealings having to do with guns.

Guns.

I've been around guns a bit, since Pops buys and sells them. For him, it's always been a necessary part of his business and why he got a firearms license. There are a lot of guns out there, and when people need money, they can be converted into quick cash.

But there were never more than two or three locked in a case behind the shop's counter. And Niko is talking about a shipment.

How much is in a shipment?

I drop off the cocktails the bartender waved me over for and nearly run smack into Vadik.

"Oh. Excuse me," I say with a polite laugh.

But he doesn't move out of my way, as if he meant for us to collide.

Such an odd man.

"Come to my office, please," he says.

CHAPTER FORTY-EIGHT

I look around the lounge. If I leave, will Dominika be mad?

"Don't worry," Vadik says. "The customers can get their own drinks from the bartender until the next girl clocks in."

"Okay," I say, and raise my eyebrows at the bartender, who nods back at me like everything is business as usual.

Which I guess it is. If nothing's ever truly normal, then there's no non-normal. Right?

I follow Vadik to his office and on the way, Dominika catches up. She glares at me, but Vadik shuts her down.

"Leave it, Dominika," he growls without slowing his pace.

Well, shit.

I turn my back to her, pleased she can be over-ruled, and trot a couple steps to catch up to Vadik who, truth be told, is only slightly less intimidating than his club manager.

What is it about this guy? I'm well aware how the Alekseev brothers are selling me like I'm not even human, but Kir and Niko have… a certain humanity about them.

Vadik, not so much.

After we enter his office and he shuts the door, he takes a seat behind his massive desk, spotless save for a couple sheets of paper and two large computer screens. He leans back in his chair.

He does not invite me to sit.

Fine. He wants to be the alpha dog here. He's welcome to it. I have no illusions that I am, or ever will be, at the top of the pack around here. Nor do I want to be.

He tilts his head before he speaks, as if to disarm me. Maybe to prove he does hide a bit of charm beneath that flinty exterior.

Not buying it.

"Seems as if you like my brothers. Especially Niko."

I look at him, unsure how to reply. I wouldn't say I particularly like Niko or any of the guys, knowing what they are about to do with me. I prefer to hate them in fact, but I'm not sure I'm pulling that off, either.

Vadik continues. "I noticed you turned to him just a while ago, with your concerns about Alexei."

Oh. That.

"I… I did. I wasn't sure what else to do. I'm sorry if that's out of line. It's just that the man scared me. And I guess I thought that since you protected me from Dimitri that maybe…"

My words taper off. These guys aren't going to do shit for me. The only reason they tussled with Dimitri was for the power play. I'm of no importance aside from being a pawn in that game.

Vadik leans onto his desk, putting his hands together as if in prayer. But he's not praying. Just posturing. "I'm not upset with you, Charleigh. It's not a problem, your asking for help when you need it."

Okay. Is he for real, or just fucking with me? Because he seems pissed off.

Or is he jealous?

Since I'm not sure, I keep quiet.

"We have some shit going down here, Charleigh. Things might seem tense over the next few days. Maybe longer."

Whoa. Is he confiding in me?

Why would he do that?

"Niko… told me something about guns," I venture. I'm not interested in their business dealings, but I can pretend to be.

Vadik nods. "Dimitri's men have been back to the club, bragging about messing with my brothers and me."

My ears perk up at this information. Can I find an opportunity to add to their drama?

Vadik laughs for a split second, and then shakes his head like he can't believe Dimitri's stupidity.

"They have?" I ask, hoping he'll say more.

What does this mean for me? And why is he telling me?

I continue before he can answer. I can't help it. "Vadik, are they going to buy me? Or try to? What about that man… Alexei?" I ask, my voice shaking.

He looks down, avoiding my gaze, which says it all.

He doesn't give a shit about what happens to me, and yes, they're selling my ass.

"You'll kill me," I whisper. "You're sending me off with some horrible, dangerous, crazy men. I'll end up dead somewhere, and you don't care. You're no better than my father. Actually, you are worse."

I'm not normally one to poke a bear. But I want to do something to Vadik. I want to hurt him like he's going to hurt me. And if I only have words, that's what I'll use.

But instead of being angry or insulted, the corner of his mouth crooks up into some sort of demented smile.

He likes it. He likes that I threw some vehemence his way. I wish I had more. *He* wishes I had more.

"I get it," he says. "I wouldn't be happy to be in your shoes either."

As much as my high heels are killing me, I straighten up and pull my shoulders back. I might be powerless. But I have self-respect. And I didn't have to spend money to get that, like the other clowns around here.

"Vadik, can you and your brothers buy me?"

CHAPTER FORTY-NINE

Vadik

My office is silent for an unusual length of time after Charleigh's question, the only sound an old industrial radiator snuffling along under one of the windows lining the wall behind me.

When this was my father's office, he positioned his desk so he could see out the window. I was never exactly sure why because there isn't much of a view in this part of town other than some derelict, abandoned warehouses and weed-infested parking lots.

I never got to ask him, but perhaps he liked watching the members as they came in? Which doesn't make a lot of sense because we have cameras everywhere anyway, and he could just watch them on his computer monitor.

When Uncle Mikey took over, he didn't change a

thing, partly because he hardly spent any time here. Dominika ran the show for the two years Mikey was looting it, and she has her own closet of an office near the girls' dressing room, since they've always been her main responsibility. Why my father didn't give her a better office, like one with a view since there are plenty to choose from, puzzled me until I realized hers was an easy place for their daily trysts. No windows, fairly soundproof, and deadlocked from the inside.

What every man wants for his mistress, I suppose. If that's your thing.

So when Mikey split and I moved in, I changed shit up a bit by turning my desk to face the door. Why anyone would ever have an office with their back to the door is beyond me, even if you're not in my kind of business. You're so vulnerable like that and even if you don't have safety concerns, every time someone comes to your office you have to turn around to see who it is.

Plus it's bad feng shui or some shit.

"Come have a seat over here," I say to Charleigh.

I intentionally take the big leather easy chair, leaving the sofa for her so she doesn't assume I'm making a move on her.

"You want a scotch, Charleigh?" I cross the room to get myself one.

When she doesn't answer, I see she's sitting on the edge of the sofa, explosively tense, with her hands folded over her knees. The prim and proper bearing is a funny juxtaposition to the sexy little costume she wears for cocktailing.

"Well?"

She takes a deep breath and slowly releases it, her cheeks adorably puffed out, revealing her ambivalence.

"I've… I've never had scotch."

Well, damn. Why didn't I realize that? She's not the typical party girl I cross paths with. Why would I think any different? She's probably an aficionado of cheap light beer and the occasional five-dollar bottle of wine. Special occasions only.

I pour her a small amount and add an ice cube. This sort of thing goes down easier, at least for the first time, when it's been chilled first.

"Here you go," I say, helping myself to a seat next to her. I realize I should probably give her some space, but fuck it.

She attempts to take the glass from me, but I nudge away her hand, raising the drink to her lips myself.

Like I'm feeding her.

"Just take one tiny little sip, pretty girl."

She glances sideways at me, her face full of

distrust, and parts her lips to accept the rim of the glass. A small sip of the amber liquid flows into her mouth, and as soon as she has a taste, pulls her head back and pushes the glass away.

"Ugh," she sputters, taken aback by the initial burn, repeatedly licking her lips like she lost a layer of skin.

I have to try not to laugh.

"Look. This is how you do it. You open your mouth and let it pour in. If you let it sit on your lips, it's going to burn. Now watch me." I take a smaller than usual swig so I don't freak her out, but I do let the scotch pour into my mouth as I described.

The heat is soothing and delicious. Hell, I can drink this stuff all day.

It's a wonder I don't, since I'm basically surrounded by it as well as all other forms of alcohol.

"Ready to try again?"

She frowns. "Maybe. If I can hold the glass myself."

I hand it over. "Be my guest."

She looks at the dark alcohol and takes another sip, this time bypassing her lips, at least as best she can. Taking a mouthful, she quickly swallows. She only coughs a little this time and wipes her mouth with the back of her hand.

"There you go," I say, returning to my seat.

She sits back on the sofa, visibly relaxed, I don't know whether from the alcohol, getting more comfortable with me, or both.

"Are you going to answer my question, Vadik?" she asks, her eyebrows raised expectantly.

"About?" I know full well what she's referring to. I'm just being a dick.

"My auction. I'm asking you to help me. Either you guys buy me, or make sure someone nice does."

I don't blame her for asking, and in fact respect that she has. I'd do the same in her situation. But I don't know that I can help. The wheels are already in motion and things may be out of my hands.

But there's no reason for her to know that.

CHAPTER FIFTY

VADIK

"I have to think about that, Charleigh. Right now we're having… problems, as I think you know."

She looks disappointed but nods to show interest. "Yes. Niko mentioned it."

"Dimitri's gang is up to no good, as usual. They are interfering with our businesses as well as making up shit and spreading rumors like our girls have diseases."

I have to laugh at that middle-school-level tactic. Our girls are the cleanest in the business. I have a freaking doctor on retainer to ensure just that.

"He'll do anything to take us down, that's how badly he wants the club. The man's playing with fire. And I am afraid he's about to get burned. Very badly."

"Are they trying to get back at you for telling him I was hands-off?"

Damn, she's direct. I like that.

"In part, yes. His ego is as fragile as an eggshell. But it's more than that. Years of what he sees as petty insults. That sort of thing."

She shakes her head with a little laugh. "And here I thought my life, studying for my bookkeeping cert and keeping my little sister on track, was a lot. I never worried about people turning on me. At least until my father did."

She sighs, lost in thought, and before she even sees me coming, I am back across the room sitting next to her. She's barely touched her scotch after her initial couple sips, so I take the glass from her, the ice now melted, and belt back what's left.

I'm not surprised she doesn't like it. It's an acquired taste, and something I like because it smooths out my rough edges.

Charleigh has no rough edges. At least not yet.

And then, because I can't help my goddamn self, I take a hank of her silky hair and bring it to my nose with the inhale of a man starving for oxygen.

The kind only Charleigh can deliver.

And fuck, she smells good. Girls like her do, and without even trying. She's not drowning in lotions and potions like the other women I know, guilty of trying too hard or following someone's arbitrary instruction about what attracts a man.

I wish I could tell these women, it ain't perfume.

But Charleigh. Clean and fresh, like simple drugstore soap and shampoo, and maybe a nice little hand cream.

I know I warned my brothers about this sort of thing, consorting with Charleigh. And now look at me.

I'm a damn hypocrite.

And I don't give a fuck.

I remove a clip at the back of her head and her hair tumbles forward, partially obscuring her face. She looks down, hiding behind it like a veil, so I push it aside and turn face toward me.

"Don't block me from seeing that face, pretty girl. I won't allow that. Not at all."

Her gaze meets mine, her eyes heavy-lidded and relaxed, and while I know I shouldn't be doing this—regardless of what my brothers and I have already done—I can't help myself, dammit.

CHAPTER FIFTY-ONE

I hate that. I hate that my resolve is not stronger. But I love that I'm here right now with this beautiful woman on the sofa in my office, who looks like she's about to melt into my arms.

The goddamn irony of it all.

It's been a long time since I've laid eyes on a woman who caught my fancy. I mean, I see women I want to fuck, and I often do, but they aren't anyone I'd take out to dinner or see a second time. I can't imagine trying to talk to them over a glass of wine, these women who pretty much look at me like a walking wallet, and who I pretty much look at as a way to empty my balls. We each get what we want, more or less, and go our separate ways.

Then there's Charleigh. She has so much to offer,

and yet she'll be gone in a few days. I will never see her again. Do I know what will happen to her? To an extent, I do. Men, insatiable men who are ruled by their dicks, will spend ungodly amounts of money to take from her something no one else but they will ever have. It's an obsession for some, deflowering a virgin, ruining her so no one else can have the part of her that they claim. That's winning to them, and winning is everything. No matter the cost.

We know this about these men and exploit it to the fullest. We're just fulfilling basic human needs, a solid business strategy that's been successful for years and will continue to be. Strippers, gorgeous girls delivering drinks—and auctions—will get the club back on solid ground after Uncle Mikey's damage.

My brothers have asked *why*. Why do I care so much about a business of ours, the club, which is not nearly as lucrative as our liquor stores, gambling rooms, and security services, not to mention the international 'cargo' we move? The club takes time out of our days and nights, requires us to deal with no end of assholes, and then there is Dominika, who's difficult on her best day.

I have my reasons, and I am far more committed to them than Kir or Niko. First, this club was Papa's pride and joy. It's where he mixed with his friends, and where he negotiated business. Established himself in America, which brought him no end of happiness. It's not easy to leave your home country, even when there's a price on your head, as there was on his. With one foot in the old world and one in the new, he missed Russia terribly, but seldom looked back when he had so much to look forward to.

The second, and perhaps most important reason I am keeping the club alive, is that I will seek revenge against Dimitri for the murder of my parents. At some point he'll trip up, and by keeping him close at hand here at the club, we'll be front and center when he does. The man is not smart, so it's just a matter of time. He'll step right into the trap we've set and the only way he'll get out is by chewing off his leg. Something I can't wait to witness.

Charleigh will soon be gone from our property, our lives, and our lustful imaginations. She stirs something in me, but is not meant to be mine. Or my brothers'. She is here to serve another purpose. Where she ends up, I will likely never know. It's not my job to follow her. I'll be on to the next auction girl in no time, and this one will be a distant memory.

Or will she?

I need to get my ass back behind my desk instead of feeding Charleigh scotch. I need to do some work, starting with the crisis *du jour*—the missing gun shipment. I need to stay away from this woman who, as much as I might like her to, will never have the chance to heal my scars. She won't be around long enough, and who knows if she would even want to get involved in my darkness, anyway.

If she's smart, she won't.

But instead of being the wise, older brother to Kir and Niko and walking away from Charleigh like I told them to, I slowly pull her closer, closer until I can brush my lips over hers, back and forth, teasing and igniting the passion I suspect lives right under the surface of her respectability.

Other men want to ruin her. I want to cultivate her, like a garden exploding into a symphony of color and fragrance until it takes your breath away. You know you've lived nirvana, tasted the best life has to offer, and it no longer matters what happens after. You've been on top of the world. There's nowhere else to go.

And that's okay.

Such an indulgence is not meant to be, though, especially not for me. I carry too much ugliness, and there are too many fractures in my character that no amount of Charleigh can redeem. If I could clone her a hundred times, it would not be enough.

And that's why she must go.

Until she does, however, I will make her feel like the princess she is. I suspect she's not been treated like one many times in her life, if ever, and after she leaves our property, she probably won't be, either.

I know I can't fuck her, that would be entirely too greedy and counterproductive, but there are other pleasures I can bring her.

And many she can bring me.

"Such a beautiful girl." I trail my kisses down her neck and into the cleavage created by her tight bustier.

I move down between her legs and, parting them, push up her short skirt, pressing my face into the crotch of her panties to take a long inhale of her sweet aroma. This is mine, all mine, at least for the moment. I slide the thin fabric covering her pussy to the side, and out pops her little pink clit, greedily demanding attention, and even more so when she shifts and pushes her hips into my face.

Message received.

I slide my hands under her bum, grabbing her panties and pulling them down until they rest around one ankle. I push her wide open again and swipe a finger up her wet slit. She gasps and shivers, and my dick is so hard it hurts inside my trousers.

Fucking hot.

"Baby," I whisper. "Show me how you touch yourself."

Her head pops up off the sofa and her eyes widen, studying me as if she's not sure whether I'm serious. When she doesn't move, I take her hand and place it between her legs, leaving it there to see what she does.

She might be a virgin but I am sure she masturbates. How do I know? There are cameras in her bedroom, and she plays with herself most nights before she goes to sleep.

God love her.

With her gaze locked to mine, she teasingly slides a finger between her bare lips, reaching all the way to her ass cheeks, then brings it back to her clit, which she circles with two fingers.

I stand between her parted legs and reach to open my trousers. With the weight of my belt, they clatter to my ankles, and I lower my boxers enough to free my aching cock.

She stops her little circles when she sees it, not sure what's next, and looks up at me, her eyes hooded, her mouth full and wet.

She's not afraid. Just curious.

"Keep going," I say, stroking my length from root to tip.

I slide my hand over my hard-on, up and down, while she looks, and I watch her play with her pussy.

She twitches, and her hand speeds up. Her mouth opens slightly, but she keeps her eyes on my dick. Fuck all, I could come right here all over her. But she needs to come first.

Then I'll spill my seed.

"C'mon, baby," I whisper, "stroke that clit. Make yourself come."

As if my demanding words push her to the edge, her hand moves faster. A second later she's shaking, strange, guttural sounds flying out of her mouth. Her hips buck off the sofa to push harder into her fingers.

That's all I need. I lean over her and spurt my cum right onto her pussy, watching it run off her hand and between her slightly-parted lips.

"Oh fuck, yeah," I growl, emptying the last of my load.

With one arm, I lean onto the sofa and attempt to catch my breath. As I do, she brings her hand up to her mouth and licks the mixture of our juices off one finger and then another.

Holy fuck, I am in trouble.

CHAPTER FIFTY-TWO

CHARLEIGH

Vadik closes up his trousers and brings me a towel from his bar cart. I wipe my hands and everything he got all over me and catch him staring like he's never seen a woman.

What a strange man. So gruff and cold, and yet craving connection like a lost child. It's maddening. And kind of tragic.

"Hi," I say, and we both laugh.

He breaks his awkward stare and points toward the corner of his office. "There's a bathroom over there."

I kick off the panties around my ankle and ease down my skirt—at least as far as I can, since it's so damn short. It's funny, just a few days ago I wanted to die of embarrassment to be dressed so immodestly, and now I don't even notice anymore. As if I've been wearing clothes like this all my life.

In all the excitement, my shoes came off, so I pad across Vadik's plush carpeting in my stockinged feet to the bathroom, moving silently. Maybe I should just go back to my own room and get cleaned up, but I want to at least be somewhat presentable before I leave his office. I guess it will come as no surprise to anyone, given the nature of the club and my role here, but I still default toward being somewhat private. I imagine at some point, I won't care about that anymore, just like I don't care that I'm walking around half-naked. Who knows.

I shut myself into Vadik's bathroom and grab a thick towel, the same kind someone keeps replacing in my own bathroom, and splash water on my face. I finger-comb my hair and pull my panties back on after cleaning up down there. Keeping the water running at a trickle, I put down the toilet lid and take a seat to catch my breath and clear my head.

How I feel close to someone who is about to ruin my life is beyond me. It's fucked up on so many levels. And yet when we were coming together, we were *connected*. Like really connected. I could feel his orgasm, and I swear he could feel mine.

Elbows on my knees, I put my head in my hands and force a couple deep breaths. The confusion and conflicting thoughts bouncing around my mind are horrendous, and the grief I want to give myself for being intimate with such a man—his brothers included—is crushing.

If I come out of this alive, will I end up hating myself?

And wouldn't that be the worst thing of all? To lose my self-respect? To loathe nobody more than myself?

I shake the thoughts away. I just have to get through today.

Over the sound of the trickling faucet, I hear Vadik's office door fly open, and I immediately identify the loud voice that follows as that of Kir.

"Looks like someone had fun. Did Cinderella run away and leave her glass slippers behind?" Kir asks, laughing.

Dammit, I left my shoes by the sofa.

Vadik responds evenly. Like always. "Fuck off, man. What do you want?"

"Hey, Niko needs some reinforcements. Let's go."

"Why? What's going on?" Vadik asks.

"Not sure, but I think he has a lead on the cargo and wants to confront Dimitri with some backup."

With my ear pressed to the door, I hear some clicking, which I can only imagine is the loading of a pistol.

"Hey," I say, bursting out of the bathroom.

I run to the sofa and put my shoes back on.

"We're heading out, Charleigh," Kir says, Vadik following him to the door.

"I know," I say, tagging right behind them.

I have no plan. I just want to see what I'm involved in. And up against. As long as they'll let me.

Vadik and Kir stop in their tracks, first looking at me and then each other as if each is waiting for the other to tell me to go back to my room.

Neither says a thing.

CHAPTER FIFTY-THREE

Charleigh

I follow Vadik and Kir out the building and we climb into the back of a big, dark SUV with a driver up front. I look back at the warehouse and spot Dominika looking out the window, watching me leave with the guys as the driver floors it and hits the road.

This is going to chap her ass, for sure. And the best part is, she knows she can't say a thing.

"Do you think Niko's in over his head?" Kir asks his brother as if I'm not even there.

They are totally ignoring me, which is just fine.

I can't believe they let me tag along, and figure if I don't draw attention to myself and keep quiet, they'll forget I'm here. I have questions, but file them away for later.

Vadik takes a deep breath. "He may be in too deep. You know, he's new to some of this shit. He hasn't been at it as long as you and me. Papa protected him for a long time. Niko will catch up, but Dimitri can be formidable when he has his shit together. The fucker is determined unlike anything I've ever seen. He won't stop until he's dead."

A cold shiver runs over me the way Vadik speaks so casually of death. Just another day at the office for the Alekseev brothers, I guess.

"Do we know for sure Dimitri's people intercepted the shipment?"

Vadik looks out the window as we pull into a parking lot not unlike the one at the club—sprawling, overdue for maintenance with large cracks and potholes, and all the cars parked at one end, closest to a run-down warehouse like theirs.

"Who else could it be?" Vadik asks. "It's not the authorities, we've already had our contact check on that. And other than them, who would be stupid enough to mess with our shit? The *Pakhan* is not going to be happy. There's been a lot of pressure to keep the peace in order to maintain our low profiles. Dimitri is getting close to fucking all that up."

Why haven't they gone to the *Pakhan* to resolve this issue, then? Isn't that what he's for?

I have so many questions. But now is not the

time. I follow Vadik's and Kir's gaze to a handful of men gathered around a truck. While I can't hear exactly what they're saying, voices are loud and there is a lot of hand gesturing. And in the middle of it are Niko and Dimitri.

Dimitri. Will he help me out of my situation?

The SUV stops and Kir and Vadik start to climb out. Before the door closes after them, Vadik turns to me. "Stay in there, Charleigh. No reason for you to leave the car."

The door slams and the locks click into place right away. I turn to look at the driver, and he nods back at me, confirming he's taking his orders from the brothers and no one else.

Including me.

It takes only a moment for things to get so heated among the men that the driver leaves the SUV, I suppose to provide reinforcement. When he does, the doors unlock. And they don't re-lock. I remember Vadik's words, that I have no business getting out of the car. But that doesn't mean I can't listen. I open my window a couple inches since the key is still in the ignition, but I can't fully make out what they're saying.

Until I hear my name mentioned. Yeah, I definitely hear my name.

Vadik, in clear view, has his hands spread out like

he's trying to reason with someone. His brothers are frowning, concentrating, anticipating, and Dimitri wears his usual mocking sneer. They are all so engrossed, they'll never notice me exit the far side of the SUV, the side they can't see, where I can crouch down behind a tire and listen better.

I even contemplate escaping for a moment, but picture the hell that would rain down on my father and, by default, Evie. I'm not so concerned about Pops, not anymore, but Evie's a different story. She has her life ahead of her, and while she's messing things up right and left, I have to believe it's just a phase she'll find her way out of.

She needs me for that.

But first things first.

I open the car door slowly and carefully slip out, staying low. Then, I move to the end of the car where I can crouch beside the wheel, and try to make sense of the conversation I overhear.

"I don't know why your men blame me for everything that goes wrong in your business. Maybe you should have learned from your father's success. He never had these issues you boys do," Dimitri says, taunting, poking, pushing.

Does he have no idea how dangerous his behavior is? Or does he just not care? It's like he has a death wish.

I hear a sharp intake of air, and while I can't see, I know it's one of the brothers trying not to lose his shit on this creep. "Don't bring my father into this, you fucker. In fact, don't ever mention him again with that dirty mouth of yours."

These guys aren't kidding when they say they hate Dimitri.

But I guess that's how you are if someone killed your parents and got away with it.

CHAPTER FIFTY-FOUR

CHARLEIGH

That's when I feel a sharp tug on the ponytail I fixed my hair into after messing around with Vadik. The pain is so sudden and sharp, I emit a small scream in spite of all attempts to remain silent. I am yanked to my full height so fast I can't get my feet under me. I'm essentially hanging by my hair, scrambling to grab anything within reach.

But there is nothing for me to grasp as my attacker drags me away from the car. My scalp screams in pain as it and my hair support my body weight, and I wonder how long it will take before it begins to rip out of my head. They've done this before, I can tell. This person who's grabbed me is well aware their torture is crippling. I swing my arms frantically but only flail. Hell, even if I had a weapon, I'm not sure I could think clearly enough to use it. But, of course, if I had a weapon, this might not be happening.

"Well, well," Dimitri booms from where he stands with the brothers.

I'd know that voice anywhere.

My attacker drags me from the hidden side of the SUV to where the rest of the men are. Dimitri and his sidekicks laugh, while the Alekseevs, each of the three, go from wearing angry, tight expressions to murderous rage.

Is that because of a sense of protection or responsibility they feel for me, or just that Dimitri thinks he's bested them?

"What the fuck—" Niko says.

"She must have been waiting in the SUV, boss," my handler calls to Dimitri. "I caught her listening."

The man hauls me in the direction of the guys, and because I still don't have my feet solidly under me, I'm tripping and stumbling like a drunk person.

"Let me go," I scream, continuing to flail, more out of reflex than any hope it will help.

I picture my hair coming out in chunks, my thrashing and screaming making the pain worse, and yet I don't surrender.

I can't expect anyone to help me. I have to look out for myself.

Then, all at once, the agony ceases. The tugging, the suffering, and especially my screaming come to a complete halt, not because the pain is over, but because the breath is knocked out of me. I've been dropped onto the hard asphalt below, which I crash into like a deadweight, scraping the shit out of one of my shoulders. While my scalp still burns, the worst of it has subsided. I am now lying in a crumpled pile of my own limbs, my face pressing into the gritty, rocky parking lot surface.

Blinking, I look up and the first face I see is Dimitri's, his eyes narrowing like a serpent's about to dig its fangs into its prey. Should I reach for him? Can I add fuel to this already-burning fire.

But Niko is at my side, hoisting me up and giving me time to catch my both my breath and my balance.

When I am finally steady on my feet, he still doesn't let me go. The urge to burrow into him, to slide under one of his arms and pull it the rest of the way around my shoulder, is strong, but so is the itch to grab the pistol from the waistband of his trousers and make all of them suffer.

But I do neither. One, I don't show my need for comfort because I don't want Dimitri to know he can get to me, and two, I don't shoot anyone because I know I'll end up dead too.

"And there she is, the lovely Charleigh. Tell me,

darling," Dimitri croons, "how is your papa? And your little sister, Evie?"

Niko's grip tightens around me. He knows how I will react to such a comment. And, obviously, so does Dimitri.

I force my expression to stay neutral, but a burning that begins in my stomach makes its way to my throat, grinding on my insides like sharp pieces of glass. I couldn't speak if I wanted to. I can barely breathe as it is.

The bastards.

"You're okay now," Niko whispers in my ear, and the urge to throw my arms around him has never been stronger.

"I'll tell you what, gentlemen," Dimitri says expansively. "I'll overlook your accusation that I have something to do with your little shipment *problem*, if I may have this this lovely lady here at my disposal."

My voice returns. "I… I am being auctioned next weekend," I blurt, hoping this might deflate some of the tension in the air.

I should have stayed in the car. Actually, I should have stayed at the club.

Dimitri grins, showing off a gold tooth in the side of his mouth. "That's right," he says, tapping his temple. "Next weekend is the auction. How fun that will be."

My stomach flips again at the thought of his hands on me. I am not sure which is worse—him or Alexei.

They're equally repulsive in their own ways. But I force a little smile for him, anyway. I need allies and there's no telling where they'll come from.

Vadik takes a step toward Dimitri. "You will never have the chance to bid on this girl. Never."

Screeching tires distract us all, and when everyone turns toward the source, I have to fight the impulse to run. First there's nowhere to go, and second, I have no doubt all these men are armed, and I probably won't get ten feet away without a bullet in my back.

A car stops next to the SUV, and two men in dark suits and sunglasses hop out and survey the scene. Then, one of them leans back into the car and says something quietly, I am pretty sure in Russian, to someone inside. A third man steps out, buttons his jacket, and nods in our direction.

I look at Niko. "Who is he?" I whisper.

Niko straightens his back. "The *Pakhan*."

CHAPTER FIFTY-FIVE

Pakhan. From what I can tell, he's some sort of boss. Or mediator. Or maybe a combination of the two.

"Gentlemen," he says, a grave expression on his creased face.

He throws me a disinterested, cursory glance, most likely because of the state of my clothing—or should I say, lack of? To him, I'm just some bimbo club employee.

Not the cause of any problems. More a symptom of them.

The men, the Alckseevs and Dimitri's group, take turns greeting the *Pakhan* with handshakes and, I observe, a respectable amount of eye contact.

Not so different from anywhere else.

And then one of the *Pakhan's* men steps into the group. "We understand Dimitri Yegorov has a grievance, caused by an accusation by Niko Alekseev."

All the men nod.

"And that Niko has no proof. Is that correct, Niko?" the man asks.

Vadik steps up. "Wait a minute now—"

But the man cuts him off. "Do you have proof? Or no proof?"

Vadik and Niko exchange glances. "No," they say.

Both the *Pakhan* and the man look down, shaking their heads.

I don't know if I'm more fascinated by this exchange, relieved that someone is here to mediate, or scared that a brawl is about to break out.

Dimitri holds his chin up, as if to underscore the insult he's endured. "They have accused me with no proof. In fact, they have accused me of other things too. Until today, I have always been willing to let this go. But they've gone too far this time. And as payment, I want the girl," he says, gesturing toward me with his chin. "Today."

He doesn't even look at me. Just gestures. Like I'm not worth the trouble.

Okay. Maybe he won't be an ally.

The *Pakhan* turns his attention to me. "This is what you want?" he asks Dimitri, pointing.

Cripes. Like I'm not even here.

He nods. "You have permission to take her."

What?

Is this my opportunity?

The previous quiet erupts into an explosion of both protest and approval, starting with my automatic shriek. In spite of my lame masterplan, I run to hide behind Kir, on the edge of the group, and both Niko and Vadik start speaking at the same time. Actually, shouting.

A glance at Dimitri shows a smug smile as he watches the brothers, his enemies, try to change the *Pakhan's* decision.

I'm right. This has nothing to do with me. I'm just collateral damage. They could be fighting over a chair, just to see who wins.

Fuckers.

The *Pakhan* raises his hands and everyone is quiet again.

Like a schoolteacher wrangling a bunch of naughty little boys. Boys with guns. And bad tempers.

"This woman, here," Vadik says pointing, "is under contract to us. She's to pay the debt of her father and is due to be auctioned next week. We have prohibited Dimitri from attending. He lacks the… decorum of our club members. His behavior has been an affront too many times."

I don't know whether to sob with relief that Vadik is trying to get me off the hook, or sob at the hopelessness of what lies ahead.

"Please, please, please," I whisper in Kir's ear, "don't let them take me."

He reaches behind himself where I am hiding and pats my hip. I'm not comforted.

"Please," I cry, "somebody help me." The tears begin to flow.

The *Pakhan's* gaze snaps in my direction. "Quiet, girl," he growls.

The despair is overwhelming, eating me like a hungry little monster, bite by bite. My body literally hurts and I squeeze my eyes shut because I'm sure if I look down, I'll see chunks of my flesh missing, and then limbs, and then all of me will be gone.

Which might be a better fate than my current lot.

CHAPTER FIFTY-SIX

KIR

The idea of Dimitri helping himself to Charleigh —whether today or some other time—as some sort of payment over his hurt little-boy feelings?

Over my dead fucking body.

And from the expressions on their faces, my brothers feel the same way. They might not be saying much but I have no doubt about their feelings on the subject.

Brothers, yo.

I wait for the *Pakhan* to announce his verdict. For as long as I've known him, his word is final. Sure, there are times when various factions might try and sway his decisions. They are rarely successful.

But in this instance, Vadik has made a good point. There is a reason Charleigh is going up for auction, and that supersedes anything Dimitri's whiny little ass wants.

The *Pakhan* finally nods. "I see. Alright. We can resolve this later, but for now, the Alekseevs take the girl." He turns to Dimitri, whose eyes burn with rage. "She's one of their assets, given she's under contract. She goes home with them."

He considers Charleigh, looking her over like every man does, the way many will in the coming week. Dominika has distributed photos of her to drum up interest, and we are due for a record showing of parties interested in bidding on her at auction.

And yet here she is, hovering behind my left arm, completely unaware of how she has men around the globe dreaming of her. Willing to pay small fortunes, they covet her so. I have to say, I am one of them. But she is not for me. And even if having her *were* a possibility, I don't deserve her.

She is an asset to us and the club, yes. And so much more. The *Pakhan,* looking at her right now, sees that, just like all the men who attend the auction will.

His eyes drift over her, from her high-heels and ripped stockings, to her short skirt and bustier, to her face, where he takes her in, unspoiled and inno- cent as she is. He's probably wondering what we're doing with someone like her, so far from the typical woman we work with. And he certainly has a hankering for her like other men do. It's inevitable, and I wait for him to ask if he might bid on her, as well.

But he doesn't. The *Pakhan* doesn't take advantage of his position, no matter how tasty the treat being dangled before him. It's a conflict of interest, sure, to use his power for ill-gotten gains, but he's a moral man—at least as moral as bratva men can be—and he believes in earning his riches, not power-grabbing the best toy for himself.

That includes women.

"One last thing," the *Pakhan* says.

I hold my breath.

"While Dimitri can't take home Charleigh, at least not today, he is to be permitted at the auction. If he wins the girl, so be it. But you can't shut him out because of family differences. We don't do business that way."

Charleigh's grip on my arm tightens, almost to the point where it's painful.

Because there's no choice, my brothers and I nod in agreement at the *Pakhan's* directive while Dimitri fawns over him like they're the best of friends.

The *Pakhan* extricates himself from Dimitri's slimy devotions and says his goodbyes, leaving my brothers and me facing off with the enemy. I'm not at all convinced the visit accomplished much, but at least Charleigh is still with us.

Not that I, or my brothers, would have let her go anyway.

"Well," Dimitri says, smirking, "I guess no one gets what they want today."

He's right about that. I would have liked to slit Dimitri's throat today. But I didn't.

Niko, usually the calm, level-headed one, tilts his head at Dimitri, who I can see has really gotten under his skin. "Does that mean then that you *did* intercept our cargo shipment? Because it sure sounds like it."

Dimitri drops his head back and laughs, like he so often does. "It means nothing of the sort, my little Niko."

My brother's shoulders twitch just the smallest amount at the diminutive term. We all remember when Niko was small, and I'm afraid he'll never stop trying to prove he's a grown man fully capable of taking care of business. I have to remember that myself, every now and then. 'Little Niko' is no longer little.

In fact, he's a couple inches taller than both Vadik and me. Apparently, his father—his *real* father—was a very tall man.

"We will find out who intercepted our guns, Dimitri. We have many 'friends' on our payroll, who are undoubtedly far more loyal to us than you and your operations. And when that happens, there will be a high price for you to pay."

Dimitri rolls his eyes at Niko's warning, but is unable to hide the subtle shift in his expression, giving away his uneasiness with being reminded of the wide Alekseev network. His own cannot measure up to ours as a result of the respect our father garnered over the years, our cash resources, and the authorities we have in our pockets. Our shipment *will* eventually surface. When it does, there will be hell to pay.

"You're spinning your wheels, Niko," Dimitri says, clapping his hands together as if to signal the meeting's over. "I'll look forward to seeing you all next weekend at the club. I may even come a little early to get a good seat. I want to get a close look at what I'll be taking home with me. You know, since you won't allow 'try before you buy.'" He cackles at this, and Charleigh gasps.

She doesn't let go of my arm until Dimitri and team pull out of the parking lot and their tail lights fade out of sight. Then, without a word, she heads back to the SUV, crawling into the backseat. She presses her face against the window next to her and squeezes her eyes shut, like if she wishes hard enough, she'll find herself someplace else.

Anyplace else.

I jump to grab the seat next to her. She's so distracted she doesn't notice, but my brothers do and roll their eyes.

I don't care. Fuck them.

Laying an arm on the seat back, I casually stroke her shoulders, hoping I can soothe her. I won't be able to do much for her after the weekend, when she becomes the property of another man, but it feels good to do something nice now.

Or is it actually more cruel? To get her comfortable and trusting, only to foist her off on the highest bidder with no regard to what kind of bastard the man might be?

I push those troubling thoughts aside and pull her to me until she rests her head on my shoulder. Vadik and Niko are watching, unable to take their eyes off her.

God knows I need a distraction, and I figure she does too. I hate tussling with that bastard Dimitri. It's one thing to negotiate with sane people—all parties want something, you work it out, and everyone walks away with the semblance of a good deal in the end. People are happy, or at least mostly happy. But with a loose cannon like him, there's no reality check on his demands, nor is there telling when things might spiral out of control. When that happens, people end up dead.

It's likely the one to end up dead will be Dimitri someday. Not that I care. I just don't want him six feet under before we prove he murdered our parents. When that day comes, and I hope it does soon, there will be hell to pay.

Until then, we just have to suffer through the waiting game—waiting until he trips up one way or the other and reveals himself.

After a bunch of stressful bullshit like today, I like to go for a jog to clear my head. Sometimes I run for so long and so far that when I'm about dead of exhaustion and am forced to finally stop, I don't even know where I am. But since I'm stuck in the SUV heading back to the club, I am thinking of another way to blow off some steam. And maybe get Charleigh to join.

CHAPTER FIFTY-SEVEN

KIR

I gently take her chin and turn her toward me. Running a thumb over her lower lip, her mouth opens slightly. Her eyes are heavy-lidded.

Seems I'm not the only one needing some relief.

I kiss her forehead, nose, and cheeks, then brush her lips just enough to tease. It's not lost on me that when I don't fully lay my mouth on hers, she groans a little, as if in disappointment.

Hot.

But I have other plans for her pretty mouth.

"Charleigh," I whisper.

I glance at the bench seat across from me, where my brothers sit, watching intently.

"Yes?" she asks, dreamily.

"Why don't you get down on your knees here, darling?"

She pulls back and looks at me, wide-eyed with surprise. But a second later, as if she doesn't even need to think about it, she gives me a shy smile while unbuckling her seatbelt.

And slides to the car floor in front of me.

"Good girl," I say, running my palm down her cheek. "You know what I want, don't you?"

She hesitates. Maybe I said too much. Made her think about what she's doing.

Sometimes it's best not to think.

I understand the hesitation. She's with three men who are about to sell her off. How can she not hate us? How is it that she remains so civil? Would she cut my throat in the night if she could? Because I sure as hell would, if I were her.

She reaches for my belt buckle anyway.

After my Clara died, I never thought I'd be with another woman. I couldn't imagine wanting to, nor did I feel I deserved it. I couldn't even jerk off for the longest time. Pleasures of the flesh, denied to her now that she was gone, were something I had no right to, either.

If she couldn't indulge, neither could I.

My self-flagellating tendencies eventually waned,

and my desire trickled back, although not the way it had been with her. Which was fine, for a while.

Now, with Charleigh before me, I'm like a man dying of thirst, ready to do anything for a sip of water. God help anyone who gets in my way. I need to unburden myself, and the pretty girl unbuttoning my pants is going to make sure that happens.

The *Pakhan* would not be happy if he saw us now. If Charleigh is off-limits for Dimitri due to the coming auction, she's off-limits for us too.

Not that he'll ever know what we're about to do.

My pants are open and my dick springs free, thank fucking god. I thought the damn thing was going to be crushed, hard as I am inside my trousers. Charleigh, bless her, reaches into the opening in my boxers and pulls me out, and the view of her slender fingers trying to encompass me is nearly more than I can take.

She studies my cock, sliding her hand over a couple inches of its shaft, then just under the ridge of the head, and tightens her grip. I groan at the pleasure-pain, and while I want to close my eyes and let my head drop back onto the seat, I force myself to watch.

This girl will be gone from my life soon. I want to remember her.

"Go ahead, pretty girl," I say, my voice coarse, "it's okay."

I weave my fingers into her hair and slowly guide her head toward my crotch, pushing my hips to get her mouth on me sooner if at all possible.

She looks up and with her gaze locked on mine, she opens to swirl her tongue around my cockhead. A string of my precum dangles for a moment, and she uses it to lube her hand. Lowering it to the root of my dick, she strokes me there while creating a suction with her lips that is heaven.

Actually, better than heaven, because she's watching me, watching my reaction to make sure she's doing exactly what I want. So earnest. So determined.

"Baby, that's nice. Fuuuuck…," I groan.

Niko slides up behind her, pushing up her skirt and pulling her panties below her bottom. His palm, smoothing over her ass cheek, stirs something in her. She wags her bum for him as she takes me to the point where my cock bumps the back of her throat.

Love it.

For a moment, I wonder what he's going to do back there, saving her virginity as we are.

Will he fuck her in the ass? I don't think that's really Niko's thing.

But it's mine. And she'll still be a virgin.

Charleigh is pumping on my cock, her little moans adding a nice vibration. Behind her, Niko strokes between her legs. She moves her hips up and down, just like she's moving her head on my cock, and I watch my brother smile at the view beneath him.

In the next moment, my balls tighten, and while I prefer to hold it a little longer, I explode down Charleigh's throat. I haven't come this hard in a long time, and it's just what I need to bleed off some of the tightness that's been building around me, binding me like I'm in some sort of hellish straightjacket.

The SUV arrives back at the club. The driver, because he's a fucking pro, parks and gets out, leaving the four of us alone. Personally, I wouldn't mind going back inside, but Niko has Charleigh so close, there's no way he can stop now.

I move to the bench opposite and take a seat next to Vadik to enjoy the view. Charleigh is now bent over the spot I just vacated, her ass in the air and her legs spread wide. Niko is running his fingers between her lips, stroking the length of her pussy, then her clit, and then her pussy again, all pink and juicy and begging for more.

It's when her head begins to buck and she pounds on the car seat with her fist that he zeroes in on her clit, expertly rubbing it with two fingers. She pushes back for more friction and arches, tossing her head back, and emitting something between a laugh and a moan, or maybe a combination of the two.

It's music to my ears, hearing her climax, and before she's done, I have another goddamn hard-on.

CHAPTER FIFTY-EIGHT

"We have a new room for you to stay in."

While the elevator to the club's top floor *whirrs,* I hold onto its brass railing. My legs are still shaky from the run-in with Dimitri's gang and then the orgasm I had in the car. Being in close quarters with the Alekseev brothers right now does not make standing any easier. Or breathing, for that matter.

Dark, dangerous sensuality pours off each man. I should be used to it by now. Maybe even immune. And yet every time one of them touches me, it's like I've never been touched before. It's intensely electrifying. For a moment in time, nothing else in the world exists.

None of the pain, sadness, or betrayal the four of us have in common.

Maybe that's why I'm drawn to them, and they to me.

Ugh. What must they think of me? Succumbing to the charms of my captors, the ones about to send me out into the world untethered. With no concern for what will happen to me after they fatten their hungry bank accounts. It's business as usual for them, but a new level of awfulness for me.

How can anyone do something so cruel?

When it comes down to it, I don't care what they think of me. They aren't in any position to be judgmental, for cripe's sake. They are hardly without their own faults.

"A new room? Where? Why?" I ask, when the elevator opens.

What's wrong with the room I have? And why do I have to think about anything other than going to bed and sleeping for the next two or three days? I've never been so exhausted in my life.

I don't want to change rooms. I don't want to change anything. Shit, for all I know, I'm out of here this coming weekend, anyway. Can't things just stay the same until then? Is that too much to ask?

Vadik gestures for me to follow. "When we're here, staying at the club, the three of us live in a large suite. There is also a guest room. You will stay there from now on. We feel you'll be safer, closer to us."

Oh. Well, that doesn't sound so bad.

Except the 'safer' part.

"What do you mean? Am I in some kind of danger?"

Or should I be asking, *more danger than usual?* The club isn't exactly frequented by the town's most upstanding citizens. From what I know, they're nearly all criminals engaged in illegal businesses like arms smuggling, drug dealing, gambling, and laundering money, not to mention auctioning off women like me. They are never without their weapons, and regularly threaten to kill people.

Given all that, how the hell does moving me to a new room increase my safety? I've never been in so much danger in my life.

Safety is like health. You take it for granted until you don't have it anymore. You don't appreciate it, nor do you have any idea what it's like to do without it until it's too late.

The truth is, I haven't felt completely safe since my mother died. When she left, it was like she took my father with her. He was still around physically, of course, but he was just really a shell of a human being.

So, I've been in a constant state of alert since I was ten years old. Where would my next meal come from? How could I replace my hole-y sneakers? Will

I be able to get a new winter coat in time for the first snow?

Is my little sister okay?

I made it through these challenges, figuring out how to navigate a grown-up world well before my time.

But this, this shit I'm now facing is a new level altogether. One I hope most people never have to contend with. The level of uncertainty and constant threat will kill a person.

"I'm fine in the room I have, Vadik," I say firmly.

He stops and looks at me. "You are staying in the new room. All your things have been moved. This way we can keep a closer eye on you."

Are they concerned I'm going to get away? Or that someone is coming after me?

A little more information would be nice.

We go directly to the new place without swinging by my old room since I don't have to grab any of my things.

The suite is a cross between a luxury apartment and a high-end hotel room. Not that I'm familiar with either, I just spend plenty of time on Pinterest looking at fancy stuff.

And it's gorgeous, which wouldn't be so unusual if we weren't in what looks like an old, run-down building in a tired, forgotten part of town.

But incongruity has marked my life since I was dragged out of my father's shop. There's no reason for things to start making sense now.

The walls are painted a rich, dark, masculine burgundy, and the central room is furnished with oversized sofas surrounding a thick rug I'd like to dig my bare toes into. A small flame even burns in a gas fireplace, and the walls are hung with large abstract paintings. I've never seen anything like it, in person, that is.

I turn to see several doors off the main room, which must be the guys' rooms, and Vadik points to the one that's open. Guess that's mine.

"Have you guys always lived here?" I ask.

Kir laughs. "Hell no. We're just staying here while we get things settled at the club. When we can spend less time here, we'll go back to the compound."

"*Compound?*"

He nods as he pours a drink and passes it to Niko. "We own a large piece of property that we each have homes on. It's the same place our parents' home used to be. Before it caught fire."

CHAPTER FIFTY-NINE

A compound. This is news. "Was their house… completely destroyed?"

Shit. Why did I just ask that? It can't be something the guys want to talk about. But on the other hand, what do I care? It's not like I'm trying to make friends here or get a Miss Manners award for not asking tacky questions.

My mother would not approve, but then, she's not here, is she?

Niko takes a seat on the sofa and kicks his feet up on a leather-covered coffee table. "No. It was not destroyed. Not entirely. The fire was put out quickly, as it turned out. Not fast enough to save them, though. We had it torn down anyway. None of us ever wanted to go back in there."

Kir salutes with his glass of whatever, after passing me a glass of the same, which I did not ask for and do not want. "Now there's a memorial garden where their house stood. It's full of our mother's favorite flowers and trees. She and our father would have loved it."

I'd like to visit this place, not only the garden but the whole compound. I don't bother asking if I can. My opportunities to breathe fresh air are going to be few and far between soon, and I doubt these guys are taking me on any field trips between now and then after what happened today. I still wonder if I can get Dimitri to help me, but he'll have his own demands, and who knows whether they'll be worse than what I'm already facing.

I doubt I'll be doing any more sneaking out either, regardless of how badly Evie needs me. And that hurts, probably more than anything else about this nightmare. My future is as uncertain as one can be, but my sister's is even more so, and she's not even had a chance to live yet. She's just a kid.

But I keep the guys talking. Perhaps something will come of it. "You are so sure it was Dimitri who killed them."

If I'm going to be nosy, I'm going all the way.

"Dimitri has always contested that his father left the club to our dad. He's convinced the man would have wanted *him* to have part of the club. But ours became the rightful owner, one-hundred percent and Dimitri has had a bug up his ass about that ever since. He thought by getting rid of our dad he could swoop in. He had no idea Papa left the club to Uncle Mikey," Kir says.

"Not that Mikey was much better than Dimitri," Vadik adds. "He was only slightly less useless."

Kir picks up some sort of remote and clicks it in the direction of the fireplace. A huge TV screen lowers out of nowhere. "Uncle Mikey was a useless piece of shit, but he hated Dimitri just like we do. He didn't want him to have the club just like we don't."

"Why doesn't Dimitri drop it, and just focus on his other businesses?"

I'm pretty sure my kind of logic doesn't apply to this situation, but I've got to ask. It's like trying to look away from a car accident. You want to, but you don't.

"He knows the club is a cash cow for one, but primarily it's an ego thing for him. He feels fucked over."

Still doesn't make sense to me. The guy's going to get himself killed at some point.

Holy crap. Am I thinking like these people? Drawing conclusions the way they do? God help me.

Actually, I'm pretty sure God isn't going to help

me out of this situation. Nobody is. Unless I can appeal to the guys.

"Hey, Vadik," I say, "remember the other day when I asked if you guys could bid on me? So I could stay with you?"

So sad I'm asking to stay with them because they are the lesser of evils. What a freaking joke.

Not surprisingly, my question doesn't go over well.

Vadik glares at me. "Come. I'll show you your new room."

Dammit. Did I go too far?

And if I did, what the hell do they expect? Of course I'm going to try and bargain for better circumstances.

Who wouldn't? My father might be a fool, but I'm not.

For fuck's sake.

My new room is identical to the last except for some weird metal shades that look like they come down over the windows.

"Are those for blocking the sun?" I ask.

Vadik chuckles. "No. They are for blocking gunfire. This is essentially a safe room. Have you ever heard of one?"

I gulp. "Um, well, yeah. In the movies."

He nods. "Same idea. I'll let you get settled in. If

anything ever happens, that button on the wall next to the door will activate the entire system, as well as locking this door from the inside."

Lock the door from the inside?

As if he can read my mind, he shakes a finger at me. "Don't get any ideas, Charleigh. My brothers and I can override the system. So you can't lock *us* out." He rubs a hand over his smooth head like he wants to say something else. He doesn't, though.

I glance around and find not only have my few belongings been brought over from the other room, but they are creepily in the same places I left them. A magazine on the dresser. Sneakers next to the easy chair. My phone on the nightstand. I grab it and take stock of my missed calls.

First, I text Luci.

Hey there.

OMG, there u r. WTF?

Did u get an A?

Don't change subj. What's going on?

I'm fine. Rly.

Pls let me help. I know something's up. I'm begging.

Can Luci really do something to help me? Of course not. No one can help me. And telling her anything would only put her in the same sort of danger I'm in, knowing what I do about the guys.

And make things worse for me, if that's at all possible.

Sry honey, gotta go.

CHAPTER SIXTY

CHARLEIGH

I put my phone face-down on the bed. I still need to return a call to Evie, but I want to make sure I sound normal when I do.

I sprawl on the bed and stare at the ceiling.

How did my father get in so deep? What was he thinking, running up gambling debts, especially to the extent he did? Did he have no regard for how he was endangering himself? Or his family?

Did he not know there would be consequences to his irresponsibility? And how they might impact his family?

He used to be so… normal. Just a nice dad who drove us to school and helped us with our homework. Who cooked breakfast on weekend mornings to give our mom a break, and who taught us to swim at the public pool.

Then Mother was murdered.

Ten years on, he still hasn't returned to himself. I know he never will. In fact, he might be even worse now than when it first happened. He's not capable of much more than opening the store every day, doing whatever business comes his way, and going home to bed. He barely eats, certainly doesn't cook—that's left to us—and utters scarcely a word.

For most people, grief softens over time. It doesn't go away—I know that for a fact. But the broken feeling you have at the beginning loses some of its intensity. You function again. Sort of.

But Pops never came back, not even a little, even when he had a young family to look after.

It's as if guilt has eaten away at his insides...

I cover my mouth as nausea washes over me and my mouth goes bone-dry.

He...

No...

It can't be...

Never...

Did... Pops have something to do with Mother's death? Was her murder not just a random holdup, but some sort of reckoning for something he did?

Oh god. I don't want it to be true. I've lost my mother. I don't want to lose what little is left of my father. And yet if it's true, how will I ever forgive him? How do I reconcile my love for him with hate?

Mother always said people have both good and bad in them.

Further, whether he was involved or in her murder or not, will I ever forgive him for getting me in the situation *I'm* in? Hell, it might have been easier if someone had just come in the shop and shot me in the head like they did her. I wouldn't be going through this shit right now.

If that's how it all went down. Which seems increasingly likely.

I squeeze my eyes shut. I want it all to go away. Just go away.

Then I think of Evie.

As I'm about to dial her, I hear loud voices outside my room. I tiptoe to the door and listen to the guys' raised voices.

"I don't care what the *Pakhan* said, we can't let Dimitri bid this weekend."

"Jesus, Kir, I would have thought the nice blowjob you just got in the car would have you in a better mood. Pour yourself another scotch, man," Vadik taunts.

Cripes. The room might be bulletproof, but it's sure not soundproof. At least not when grown men are using raised voices.

"Fuck off, Vad," Kir says. "You know he'll stop at nothing to get her, just to show us he's in control. That he's *the man*. You know how that prick is."

"The sooner he's dead, the better," Niko adds.

I can't believe I'm listening to a conversation like this, as if these guys are normal people discussing everyday things like sports… or the weather.

But instead talk about killing people.

"I say we defy the *Pakhan*. Deal with the consequences later. I don't want Dimitri here, and I don't want his hands on Charleigh," Kir says.

"Ha!" Vadik booms. "And there we have it."

Oh my god. Has Kir taken a liking to me?

Is this something I can make work in my favor?

"You're getting soft," Vadik growls. "You both are. And it makes me sick."

I close my eyes and breathe deeply. Please, please, please…

I can't get my hopes up. It's stupid to flatter myself. These men could probably be in love with me and they'd still send me to the slaughterhouse. That's how they operate. They have no conscience. No ability to care.

They are sick, horrible people.

I don't deserve this. I don't.

My phone vibrates and because I'm tired of hearing the guys argue, I pick it up.

CHAPTER SIXTY-ONE

"Evie. Hey."

"Thanks for returning all my calls, Char," she says in full-on smartass, something she's perfected like a champ.

I wait for my irritation to pass. On top of everything else, I am not in the mood to take shit from a bitchy teenager.

"Sorry. I've been… busy. What's up?"

"Pops says you might not be coming back home."

Did I just hear a crack in her voice? Is the little monster actually upset?

And did Pops really say that? What the hell?

Now what do I say?

I don't want to lie, but I don't want to get her

hopes up, either. Poor kid has been through more than most sixteen-year-olds.

So I lie, not because it's better for her, but because it's better for *me*. Which is pathetic and lame.

"Don't listen to Pops, Evie. He's being ridiculous. But hey, while I'm gone can you do me a huge, huge favor?"

She sniffles. Shit, she really is upset, which breaks by damn heart. I'm just another person in her life who's going to let her down. "Yeah?" she asks.

"There's a lot going on for me right now, Evie. Pops too. So I need you to try really, really hard to stay on your best behavior. If you don't want to do it for yourself, do it for me. I just really need this. If you need help with anything, call Victoria. You know how she's always been there for us."

Now my voice cracks. But that's okay. I want her to know how serious I am. I can't help her the way I used to. She needs to start helping herself. She has to grow up fast, just like I did when Mother died.

"Char, what's going on? Where are you?" Evie asks in a small voice.

The voice takes me back to when she was little, when I vowed to always be there for her because our mother couldn't. She was such a beautiful little girl.

Dark curly hair and huge brown eyes. After Mother died, she was afraid to sleep alone. She held my hand everywhere we went.

She didn't want to lose me, too. After all, she'd basically just lost both parents.

I put my head in my hands. I'm not even sure who or what to hate. My father? The guys?

The world?

My shitty luck?

I end my call with Evie before I say too much, and my heart hurts so much I curl up in a ball.

Just when I'm making something of my life, this shit rains down on my head. But I can deal with these beasts. I have no choice. They're seasoned criminals for sure, but there must be some compassion, somewhere deep in their hearts. Well, maybe not Vadik's, but Kir and Niko have some humanity to them. I've got to reach that. Dig in and make a space for myself there. Make them see me as a human who deserves love and respect.

Not to be offloaded on some rich fucker so they can get their club on solid ground.

But if my father can't get his act together without selling off one of his daughters, what the hell makes me think these men are capable of major change?

The Alekseev brothers aren't nice people. They're

scarred and dangerous, damaged by the world they exist in. They have hate in their hearts.

And I'm afraid, pretty soon, I will, too.

CHAPTER SIXTY-TWO

Niko

"Charleigh. Can I come in?"

I knock on her door. She's the type who appreciates that.

Vadik and Kir left for the lounge to press the flesh with some members, but I declined. This day has kicked my ass, so I'm going to have a drink, put my feet up, and watch sports. If I don't, I'm afraid I'll punch someone's lights out, and I'm not a really violent guy.

Not compared to my brothers.

Well, relaxation *was* my plan until I overhear Charleigh talking to someone who I guess is her troublemaking younger sister.

"Come in," she calls in a weary voice.

She's beaten down. Not surprising, really.

I find her on her bed, blowing her nose and wiping away what I'm sure are tears.

"You good?" I ask, even though she's obviously not. "Want something to eat? I can get Chef to make you something."

Food is always good. Neutral. Noncommittal.

Having changed out of her work outfit, she's wearing sweats and socks bunched around the ankles. Without a sexy get-up and with her face scrubbed clean of makeup, she's unrecognizable, at least to anyone who's seen her working here at the club. She looks like any other girl who might be out running errands, picking up a coffee, or even hitting a movie.

Or whatever normal girls do. I don't know many, so can only guess.

Looking at her hands in her lap, her hair prevents me from seeing her face. That's how I know she's crying. "Not hungry," she whispers.

"Okay, then. I'll be watching sports right out here if you need anything." I start to back out of the room. I'm not sure I could really comfort her even if I wanted to. I am flat out of gas and she seems like she'd rather be left alone, anyway.

"Hey, Niko?" she calls before I pull the door shut.

"Hmmm?"

"How long… how long has my dad been coming

to your card games?" There's a brittleness in her voice I haven't heard before. Has she accepted her fate? Is the ugliness of the life we're leading her into already ruining her, turning her into something different?

It's a shame. But inevitable, I tell myself, trying to feel better about it.

I walk back into her room. "Why? Why are you asking?"

She finally looks up, and even with her red-rimmed eyes, she's still stunning. And sexy. Fuck, the way she responded to me in the car while she sucked off Kir with Vadik watching was goddamn hot. I'll be jerking myself to that sight for a good long time.

I'd better commit it to memory, because soon, she'll be out of our lives, most likely forever. That is, if Vadik has his way.

She looks around the room, gathering her thoughts. "I'm just wondering how someone like my dad gets fifty-thousand dollars in debt. That's a lot of card games. Right?"

"How do you know that? The amount of your father's debt?"

"Vadik told me."

I can see her doing the math in her head. She has no idea. Yes, it took a lot of card games for her old man to rack up that sort of debt, so sure, he played a hell of a lot of cards. But we also have games where guys lose fifty-thousand dollars in one *night*. It's all relative.

Gil Gates did not hang with the high rollers, much as he might have liked to. No, he was on the low bet tables. And he lost *a lot*. Obviously.

And yet kept coming back.

I've read it's not the actual gambling *win* that thrills people, but the setup. *Will I or won't I?* The anticipation, the suspense, the thrill and the fear. The actual winning—or losing—is just the side show. The preparation, and the hope that one's circumstances could change in an instant, is what keeps people coming back.

The promise of *more*. The promise of *new*. The promise of *reinvention*.

What they don't realize is that these are all just promises. Not guarantees.

I've seen people win large sums of money who actually look disappointed because they know that's the point where they ought to cash out and go home. And sometimes they do. But more often, they keep gambling, sometimes for days at a time, staying awake with all manner of stimulants, until they lose every last penny. It's almost a relief when this happens, because they know they get to start all over again.

A sad example of *it's the journey and not the destination*. Or however that stupid saying goes.

That's where the trouble starts. People like Gates run out of money, fast. And yes, we make loans, which only gets guys like him in further trouble. But we're not fucking babysitters. We're running a business and our players are expected to handle their own shit. A man gets in too deep? That's on him.

"It took a long time, Charleigh, for your dad to get to the point where he is now. Years and years of winning a little and losing a little. Eventually the losses outweigh the wins and that's where the debt starts to pile up. But he played for a long time. Before I was even working in the business. I mean, shit, I was still a kid when he was coming to my dad's card games."

"You remember him?" she asks, her voice rising in pitch.

"Vaguely. I used to come to work with my father. Against my mother's wishes." I laugh. "But I have a memory of you too."

She frowns. "*Me?*"

It was only two years ago but feels like a lifetime. My parent's funeral. Charleigh stood with her back to the wall, watching everything, waiting for her dad to get through the receiving line. She wasn't like the other women there, overdone and tacky. Her hair was pulled into a tidy ponytail and she wore only red lipstick with her simple dress. Vadik noticed her. We all did. It was impossible not to.

I never expected to see her again. And yet, here we are.

"My parents' funeral," I say. The one where the coffins were closed, that's how badly they were burned.

She swallows hard, the visual clearly not setting well with her. "Oh. Of course. Funny how you remember me from that day. I was trying to support Pops. He hates going to things alone."

I don't tell her that when I saw her more recently in her father's shop, I recalled how her presence at the funeral two years prior was like a breath of fresh air. Coming across her at the pawn shop, when we were trying to get her father to settle his debts, was truly bizarre. There she was, an exquisite beauty, surrounded by all the junk her father was buying and selling.

Like a rose among thorns.

And she was even more lovely than the last time I saw her.

We are quiet for a minute, each of us most likely thinking about the strange turns that life takes.

She looks at me, the new bitterness in her voice

now showing in her face. Her lips are a thin line, and her eyes are void of the light I usually see in them.

I wonder if it's out permanently.

It's bound to happen. It does with everyone involved in our world. If you don't build yourself a hard shell, you get pummeled. And Charleigh's building her shell.

I'm sorry to see this happen to her. I guess I thought she might escape unscathed. But when it comes down to it, no one's immune.

"Niko, do you think my father had something to do with my mother's murder?"

My gaze whips in her direction. Shit. I should have known at some point the story of what went down with her mother would come up. The longer she hangs around with us, the more she understands how our world works. And the more she realizes life holds few coincidences.

As she's processing this, she has questions. Lots of them.

And my mind is racing, formulating answers. I want to be careful. She's going to hear some things she doesn't like. Things that hurt. This is sensitive shit.

I study her before I answer. "Are you sure you want to talk about this, Charleigh?" I ask, settling into an easy chair in the corner of her room.

I don't want to be tempted by being any closer to her.

Yeah, right.

"Look," she starts, "you told me all about having a different dad than Vadik and Kir. You trusted me with your story. You can trust me with this."

Trust her, sure. But can she handle it? The truth?

"Okay, Charleigh," I say, knowing she will be a different person as soon as she hears my thoughts. "Yes, we think your mother was murdered because of something your father did."

I do know it wasn't by our faction. We don't take out family members. But that's all I know.

And a second later, I hate myself for telling her. It's as if I've snatched away the last shred of goodness she has.

She stares blankly. Not moving, not speaking.

Until she says, "Will you spend the night with me, tonight?"

CHAPTER SIXTY-THREE

"You're moving her again? But she just joined you in your suite yesterday."

Dominika is pissed. Pissed that we dare to show Charleigh any sort of preferential treatment in moving her out of the club and to our compound, where we will start staying again. Security is much more robust there, and we'll all be safer.

Not just Charleigh.

Things are heating up with Dimitri, and we are taking no chances.

But Dominika feels that if there are any favorites to be played, it should be her. That's how she was with my dad for years, and she is still, incredibly, entitled. While I didn't know they were together when my father was still alive, I had vague suspicions, and after my parents were gone, my brothers confirmed what I thought.

Papa's dying left Dominika high and dry. I mean, she still has her job at the club—Uncle Mikey kept her on because it meant he had to do no work, and we keep her on because the club needs the continuity that only she can provide. You'd think this would be a win for everyone, and yet Dominika still feels shortchanged, something she makes little effort to hide.

Papa didn't name her in his will. Is it wrong to leave out a years-long mistress from benefitting from your estate?

I can't really say. I can only surmise Dominika wasn't named because Papa didn't want my mother to know, in case he went first.

Which is ridiculous. As if my mother had no idea. Of course, she knew. Mistresses are a cross to bear for women like her. But he kept her spoiled, showering her with his love. And she kept her mouth shut.

To be honest, Dominika is lucky we don't can her ass, she's such a pain. But our father would not want that, and besides, she does fulfill her purpose.

Today she's especially rattled to find that Charleigh will no longer be subjected to her whims. As if Charleigh pulled one over on her. What she doesn't understand is that it's not about Charleigh, per se. The girl is a very valuable asset to the club, and there's no limit to what we will do to protect that.

To be completely vulgar, it boils down to what we can exchange for said asset. It's transactional. Nothing more. I don't like it, but that's the way it is.

Which is what makes Dominika's pettiness all the more irritating. If she understood our business at all, she'd see that. She's missing the point. It's short-sighted of her.

Personally, I may have reservations about what we're doing from time to time, but I get the importance of it. If we let Gil Gates slide on his obligations, everyone will do it. The respect our father worked so hard for will have been for nothing. When it comes down to it, respect is worth more than what Gates owes us, and more than what anyone else owes us too. It's our most valuable asset.

Charleigh is an important part of keeping all that moving forward. After all, it wouldn't do to have a failed business, especially one that flourished so well under my father. My brothers and I would look weak and ineffectual. That's the kiss of death in our world.

And yet when I look at Charleigh, I see something I think I've lost in myself. I don't know what to call it except some sort of happiness. A belief that life is fair. There's a freedom in that. A lightness. Anything is possible.

I once had that.

When Charleigh's around, I can taste it again. As if it's within reach. Attainable. Maybe even likely. And yet we're selling her. Fucking selling her.

What's wrong with this picture?

As she requested, I do spend the night with her, my arms wrapped around her slender body, and it's goddamn heaven. Her sighs and girl-snores enchant me, as does the way she flips from one side to the other and back. I've never shared a bed with someone so restless.

And yet, in the middle of the night, I wake up and we're clasping hands. She must have taken mine at some point. Or did I take hers? Without even waking, our fingers found each other's as if we've been doing it for years.

I know Vadik was dismissive of Charleigh's request that we keep Dimitri and Alexei from bidding on her. Hell, I don't blame her for asking. Alexei is a disgusting old lech and Dimitri is a loser, but those two men can provide a fuck of a lot of cash to cover what Uncle Mikey took out of the business.

That doesn't mean I'm okay with the plan as it stands, though. I'm going to do what I can to keep

Charleigh not only out of those men's hands but also out of the hands of any other club member. I just have to tread carefully. Vadik is my brother and I love him, but this is one time I won't hesitate to go against him. I don't know whether I'll win, but I'll give it my best shot. I need to proceed carefully. Make him think it's his idea. That it's for the best of the club. And all of us.

Relocating Charleigh to the compound will be a big help. In my opinion, the further we get her away from here, the more likely we are to keep her away.

And fuck Dominika. I don't care if she's bent out of shape that Charleigh's getting some sort of treatment other girls around her don't get. Is it favored? Maybe.

But Dominika has had a good ride here. She has nothing to complain about.

She better start realizing that.

CHAPTER SIXTY-FOUR

I spent only one night in the club's suite, and now I'm in the third room I've had since the guys took me from the pawn shop.

Actually, I'm in a house. A very large house. And not surprisingly, it's just as beautiful as the rooms I stayed in at the club. Actually, more so.

While there is a central house on the property, or should I say compound, each guy has his own cottage. Although they're not very cottage-y if you ask me. Each one's bigger than where my whole family lives. They are modern with lots of glass, metal, and slanted roofs. I can tell from the outside they have their own stone fireplaces. I bet they have amazing kitchens too, the kind I see of celebrity's houses on Pinterest.

I am to stay in the central house, or the 'big house,' as I have named it. It's palatial, with a gigantic, curving staircase in the foyer, and more rooms than I can count. The house is full of the fragrance of flowers, something I wouldn't expect the guys to care much about, and there are housekeepers and other staff milling about.

They smile at me politely and don't say a thing.

The guys briefly show me around and then to my room, which is even bigger and nicer than what I had at the club.

And yes, once again someone moved over my belongings, placing them just where they were in the previous room. So strange.

"Is my room here a safe room? Can I lock it like the other one?" I ask, sitting on the edge of the bed.

I have to say, these guys spare no expense when it comes to beds. This third one is just as heavenly as the first two I slept on. And the sheets are an incredible silky cotton…

But I remind myself I'm here for just a few days. Best not get used to it. Who knows what kind of hell-hole I'm going to land in on the other side. Just because the guys are auctioning me to the man who will pay the most for my virginity, that doesn't mean he's going to be using his fortune to make me comfortable.

"You don't need a safe room here," Vadik says. "We have several guards and the perimeter is secured with an electric fence."

"Wow. That was an electric fence?" I ask, thinking back to the beautiful black gate we entered the property through.

"Yup. Doesn't look like it, does it? That's the whole idea. The security team also flies drones several times a day to check things out. So you're safe anywhere on the property."

I find that hard to believe, but these guys know way more about this sort of thing than I do.

Seeing the three of them in my room, in their dark bespoke suits, simply giving me the lay of the land, seems so strangely normal. Like I'm being briefed at a new job or something. They point out this and that as if they really want me to feel at home.

I have no idea why. It's not like I'm going to become a return customer.

I wonder if Niko will sleep with me again. I have no idea what his brothers thought of our doing that, but they couldn't have been too happy about it, based on the limited conversation I overheard afterwards.

Don't get attached.

You're too soft, Niko.

Don't think with your little head. It'll only get you into trouble.

Niko, with his tousled blond hair and mixed-up parentage. At times it's unfathomable that he is part of the criminal underworld. He is sweet and kind. And makes me feel secure. The night he spent with me was a dream. I woke up in the middle of it just to take in his masculine beauty, see his chest rise and fall, and listen to him breathe. When I wove my fingers through his, just to see how it felt, his hand clasped mine right back. He didn't even wake up.

Kir has his dangerous edge, one that occasionally reminds me to watch what I say. I wouldn't want to be on his bad side. Ever. Has he always been like that? Or did the death of his beloved Clara turn him into something temperamental and cold? The first time I encountered Dimitri, Kir's sheer force in escorting him out of the club was frightening. I thought for sure he was going to kill the man. Of course, knowing what I now do, I wish he had killed him.

Yes, I am wishing someone dead. That's something I never would have done two weeks ago. I also wouldn't have given a relative stranger a blow job two weeks ago, nor pranced around in high heels and a short skirt with my behind hanging out.

No, I'd be bumming around in my ripped jeans,

Converse Chucks, and meeting up with Luci to study and plan our bookkeeping careers. We even talked about, once we got our certificates, getting an apartment together in Chicago. We figured there are lots of bookkeeping jobs in a big city like that.

Last, there's Vadik, the big brother, who's hard to read with his hot-cold personality. I'm never sure where I stand with him. Regardless, every time I see a little past his hard, outer veneer, which seldom happens, my stomach flips and my heart races. He's gorgeous in a tough-guy sort of way with his shaved head and scowling eyebrows. If I ran into him in a parking garage, I'd probably head the other way. He has *that* kind of power. It's the only way I can think to put it. I mean, when he looks at me, I could swear he sees through me. Like he knows my thoughts.

And desires.

Then there's the way they touch me. Each one sends me spinning, flying into some sort of sexy, alternate universe. Don't they feel it too? How we connect through sexual pleasure? I don't get how the hell they are so willing to just toss me to the highest bidder, like I'm nothing. Nothing to them, nothing to anyone.

Are they that coldhearted?

The bastards.

All for my virginity. Once that's gone, will I be

cast aside like some sort of trash? And why, in these men's eyes, is that the most valuable thing about me?

It's as if I—or any woman, for that matter—am nothing more than a vagina. Nothing more than my ability to provide a man with a way to pleasure himself.

How is it they think like that? Where did they learn that?

On top of everything, and perhaps worst of all, I'm madly attracted to them. I hate it. I hate that I'm weak, and I hate myself for *not* hating them, the very people taking away everything that's ever been important to me.

It's crazy and makes no sense, but I *crave* their touch. I think about it night and day. When I share a meal with them, I can barely swallow. When they're in close proximity to my bedroom, I can't sleep. When they speak to me, I don't follow the words they're saying.

The contradictions make my head spin.

I'd do anything right now to just dive into one of my bookkeeping textbooks. They are my safe place. That's what I love about the subject. It's orderly. A place for everything. Predictable. There are rules, and everybody follows them.

I am comfortable in that world. When I am immersed, I feel like I'm wrapping a warm blanket around myself. Like I've found a place where I belong. And found something I am good at.

Those days are over now, unless I can change the path I'm on.

Which will take a freaking miracle.

CHAPTER SIXTY-FIVE

CHARLEIGH

The next couple days pass uneventfully. The staff has started talking to me a little and the housekeeper even let me help in the kitchen. If they are curious about my status—where I've come from and how long I'm staying—they don't mention it.

It's almost like they've seen women come and go from the place before.

Of course they have. I'm just another number.

The thought is like a grinding pit in my stomach. *I am one of how many?*

Have they seen women like me so many times they don't care anymore? Have they lost some of their humanity, like me? Or are they totally devoid of it by this point, like the Alekseev brothers and the members of their club?

While each of the guys has his own place on the property, they meet and conduct business here in the big house, where my room is tucked away upstairs and at the end of a long hall.

And this morning, as I was getting ready to walk to their parents' memorial garden, I hear them meeting with their door open, something I've never seen them do.

When my name is spoken, I slow down.

"How many bidders will we have tomorrow night?" Vadik asks.

Tomorrow. Tomorrow, my life will essentially be over. I choke back a sob. I am so tired of crying.

Papers shuffle. "I'm going through the RSVP list right now. According to Dominika... it looks like fifty or so," Niko answers.

There's a long, low whistle, and Kir speaks up. "Damn. We've never had a turnout like that."

The auction is on. Coming like a freight train.

I feel like someone is sitting on my chest. I sink to the floor outside the guys' office, no longer able to stand. I'm actually grateful I'm having trouble breathing. Maybe things will end for me, saving me a lot of trouble.

Of course, then my dad's debts wouldn't be paid. But I wouldn't be around for that to be my problem anymore.

Crushed. That's what I am. Completely and totally crushed. I suppose on some level I thought I might get a free pass. That I'd dazzled the guys so much they couldn't bear to part with me. That I'd be the one they set free—whatever free looks like in their world.

But no. I'm still just a walking, talking bank deposit. I'm their ticket to financial stability. Nothing more.

Jesus, I'm an idiot.

What the hell did I expect?

A person is not forced to sign a contract and taken to a criminals' club by nice people.

I struggle to my feet and rush out the front door before they find me eavesdropping. As always, the guards are patrolling, so taking off is not an option.

Today is no different from any other day.

So, I head over to the engraved bench in their parents' garden.

Mama and Papa, it says.

These guys know loss. They know pain. And yet they can't empathize with me? I settle into the place where I've spent the last couple days reading books out of the guys' library, but this time I just bury my face in my hands.

To lose all hope is like having your breath stolen. It is the lowest, darkest place a person can be. It's lonely and sad and full of sorrow. So many sorrows.

That's where I am right now.

CHAPTER SIXTY-SIX

It will be one happy fucking day when I can stop thinking about the club all the time. Seriously. We guys have other businesses to attend to that are far more profitable than this vanity project we are keeping on life support out loyalty to our father. Running it is an endless, thankless task, even if we have Dominika to manage the day-to-day.

Dealing with the problems of our members, their card games, the strippers, and everybody else drains me. I am a goddamn babysitter.

Given the choice, we'd abandon the club without much thought or regret. My brothers have been willing to let it go for some time. I'm just not ready yet. Someday I will be.

But today is not that day.

We invite Charleigh down to have breakfast with us, but she declines. In fact, she's downright abrupt, not that that sort of thing fazes me, but it's out of character for her. She's usually pretty upbeat, especially considering what she's facing, and has never once been snippy. Until today. Maybe it's that time of the month or something.

It's no wonder Uncle Mikey almost ran the club into the ground and absconded with whatever money he could grab. He didn't see it as a big priority, either. In fact, he probably found it a pain in the ass that my father left it to him at all. He stuck around for two years, which I suppose in his mind completed his duty, and left the country before the authorities could nab him.

We have no idea where he's gone, although I figure we'll hear from him at some point. He'll want money or have a stupid reason to return to the US, like to get a cavity filled or something, and he'll want our help with a fake passport, disguise, transportation, and all that.

And those steps still won't guarantee the Feds won't be on his ass. If I were him, I'd never come back. The chances of getting caught are too high. But that's me.

No one ever said Uncle Mikey was all that bright.

Imagine. Getting busted when you've come into the country just to get some dental work done.

The thought makes me laugh out loud. Kir and Niko look up at me from their poached eggs. They say nothing. We all have a lot on our minds, and I'm grateful to have entertained myself for a moment. I'll share my funny scenario with my brothers another time, when they are more receptive to it.

I know what they are thinking. I can read people. I don't know how I do it or why. But others' thoughts seem to come to me.

I'd rather they didn't. I don't want to know what people are thinking. I have enough of my own shit going on. But it does come in handy. Like right now.

The guys have trepidation about the auction.

I get it. Charleigh is lovely, and we'd like to see her stick around. To be honest, I have uneasiness around it too. This is new to me. After all, I'm not much more than a heartless bastard.

I can't count the number of men I've killed, people I've forced out of business, and the number of fingers, arms, and legs I've broken.

There are a few necks in there too.

I am not a good man.

Neither are my brothers, but on the scale from good to bad, I'm closer to the bad end of the spectrum than most anyone I know.

Even Dimitri is not like me. Sure, he's a pain in the ass, but he's too stupid to really do much harm. With the way he wears his emotions on his sleeve, he has no hope of ever outmaneuvering anyone. He just doesn't have it in him, and the only reason he's stuck around for so long, rather than going off and finding a new profession altogether, is that he has his dad's money, which enables him to spend his days any way he wants.

Even when they are as unproductive as a life can get.

If you have enough money, people will tell you anything you want to hear. Dimitri is so out of his league, and so completely unaware he's out of his league due to people blowing smoke up his ass, it's almost funny.

Thus, the biggest benefit of having my brothers. Whenever I start acting like a dick, they don't hesitate to cut me down to size. Thank God.

I'd otherwise be insufferable. Or more insufferable than I already am.

CHAPTER SIXTY-SEVEN

"What's that?"

I enter Charleigh's room with a dress for her, a sexy number, even sexier than the get-up she wears when cocktail waitressing.

It's long and shimmery gold, with a slit that's meant to expose the entire leg all the way up to the hip. The front has narrow swathes of fabric to cover the breasts, and it ties behind the neck. It's all held together with a strip of fabric that wraps around the waist, sort of like a cummerbund for a tux, not that anyone wears them anymore.

"It's a dress, Charleigh. And since I've brought it up to your room, it's a safe bet to say it's for you."

Jesus, she's in a shit mood. But that's because she

doesn't know what awaits her. She only *thinks* she does.

She looks the dress up and down, then crosses the room to take a pinch of fabric between her fingers. The pinch turns into a handful, and I know I've got her. I knew she'd love the way it feels. Hell, *I* love the way it feels.

She takes the hanger from me and holds the dress at arms' length, touching it, turning it, even looking inside it. Christ, she's inspecting it like it's something she's going to eat.

But when she looks back at me, her eyes are dull and flat. I don't like that we've done that to her. "Want me to try it on or something?" she says, bored, like she has nothing else to do.

I look around her room and see a book on the floor next to her easy chair. I guess she *is* bored. All she's been doing all week is reading. That and walking around the property, especially my parents' garden.

How do I know this, when I am working nonstop? First, there are cameras everywhere. And second, both the household staff and security regularly report to me what she's been up to.

They think it's a safety thing. But truth be told, I'm interested in what she does with her time. How she reacts to things. Which books she selects.

Fuck, I'm just interested in *her*.

She comes out of her walk-in closet wearing the dress. Because I didn't bring any high heels for her to try on with it, she's walking on her toes, loping across the room like a giraffe.

Regardless of her stilted demonstration, the effect she has on me is devastating. I actually get a lump in my goddamn throat, and I don't think I've cried since I was told my parents died.

The dress floats down the front of her body like someone painted her in gold. It clings to her small breasts just enough to show their shape, but not enough to show everything. Her nipples protrude in the cool room like little gold nuggets.

I twirl a finger to get her to turn.

I'll be damned if the back of the dress isn't even better than the front. She's totally bare down to the back of her waist, the dress's sash draping perfectly around her hips. The fabric glides over her ass cheeks just enough to show a little jiggle when she walks.

The embodiment of flawless perfection, that's what she is.

What every man wants. And few can afford.

"Charleigh, I'm not going to tell you how beautiful you look, because I'm sure you know. But I have something to talk to you about."

She releases an exaggerated sigh, followed by rolling her eyes.

This is like a strike to the heart. My mother, my long-suffering mother, putting up with my father's dalliances and other bullshit, used to do the same thing.

Clearing my throat, I force myself to look away, thinking back to how a lifetime with my father nearly wore her down. But she still loved him. I was told when their bodies were found, they were holding hands.

Is it too late for Charleigh? Have we completely worn her down? Ruined her? Put out the bright light that has enchanted my brothers and me since she arrived?

"Come here, darling," I say, surprising myself with the tenderness in my voice.

Her gaze glued to mine, she crosses the room, no longer on tiptoe. She holds a bunch of fabric to avoid tripping.

"Yes?" she says defiantly when she is inches from my face.

She is not mine. And yet she will be. There's no turning back now.

I reach behind her neck and untie the dress. It tumbles to her waist, leaving her breasts bare, and slides the rest of the way to the floor once I loosen the sash.

Before me stands a naked beauty, like Botticelli's Venus or some such, the sort of vision that steals away all your words and even your breath. The kind that makes time stop while you just look at it, your gift, until you tire of it.

Although you know you never will.

CHAPTER SIXTY-EIGHT

She is devoid of the shyness she had when we first played around. Perhaps someone has gotten to her before me?

No, that's not possible.

She's been better-guarded than the gold in Fort Knox.

She's mine, goddammit. She'll never be anybody else's.

I back her up until she's forced to sit on the bed.

"Take out my cock."

She swallows and looks up at me, her eyes wide. Do I see some of her light coming back? Is she waking from the dark place where she's been?

Slowly, agonizingly slowly, she pulls the stiff leather on my designer belt and opens my trouser hooks and fly. Pushing aside my shirt tails, she pulls down the waist of my boxers and reaches for my erection. I stop breathing, waiting for her hand, as if I've been craving it all my life.

Maybe I have.

Her fingertips run up and down my length, and she touches the drop of precum on my cock like she's never seen it before. Gripping me lightly, lightly enough to leave me in agony, she slides down my shaft all the way to the root. I push forward, into her face and rub my cockhead on her cheek.

There she sits, below me, her eyes closed and legs parted enough that I can see her erect clit poking out of her pussy lips.

Is this woman real? I don't see how she can be.

I reach down for her little tits, her nipples upturned and delightfully alive, and knead and pull them until she quietly moans. Without a word, she looks up at me, releases my cock, and slides back on the bed, her legs open just wide enough to let me see her, but not enough for me to slip between them.

That's okay.

Pushing my pants below my ass, I join her on the bed, nudging her legs apart to position myself between them. I push her knees up gently, tilting her pelvis into the perfect position.

I know it sounds cheesy, but if I died right now, I

wouldn't care. This is the most perfect moment of my life.

I press my cock against her opening. Her precious opening. The one we are—correction, *were* —going to auction to some fucker sick enough to want to see a virgin bleed.

"You good, baby?" I ask, just hovering.

Her eyes are half-closed and her lips are full and pink, just like her pussy. "Yeah."

"What do you want, Charleigh?" I whisper, wondering how long my control will last.

She looks at me, her hair fanned out around her head like a fucking mermaid. She reaches for my ass and digs her nails into me, propelling me forward.

I know she wants what I want. But I want her to say it. Say it out loud for both of us, like she's blessing this thing we are giving each other.

In a barely discernible whisper, she answers. "Fuck me, Vadik. I want you to fuck me."

I'm not one for virgins. I get no rush out of being someone's first, some guy a woman will supposedly remember and talk about for the rest of her life. I don't need that honor. It's a messy business, and I don't mean just because of the possibility of blood. There's this vulnerability, this fragility, that any decent man should feel responsible for. Not that many do.

I haven't.

But I do want Charleigh to remember me. Years from now, when she's doing whatever she's doing, I want her to think back, maybe even smile, and recall the strange circumstances under which she met a man like me. I want her to remember that I fucked her with care, that I made her come, and that she felt beautiful afterward.

And loved.

Fuck. I did not just say *love*.

"Guide me."

There's no way I'm going to slide into her tight pussy without a hand to steer me.

I push lightly, rocking against her, giving her time to open. She's soaking wet, so that should help, and when I enter her a couple inches, she gasps, then her head falls back on the bed, and she arches her neck.

"You okay?"

She swallows hard and nods. "Yeah. I like it."

"Can you take more?" I ask.

I've never fucked someone so politely before. What is this woman doing to me?

She nods.

I enter her slowly, so very slowly, in a steady movement until I'm balls deep. She winces and gasps, and I wait, giving her time to adjust. I want to pound her pussy, and it's taking all the self-restraint I have to hold back.

Not to mention hold my orgasm. I want to unload in her, coat her insides with my cum. But not yet.

When her nails dig into my ass again, announcing she wants more, I slide in and out, watching her for signs of pleasure or pain. A small smile crosses her lips and I pump faster, cupping her ass with one hand, and her face with the other.

Her hands slide to her breasts, running her thumbs over her nipples like I did, and I take heady pleasure in the thought that I might have taught her something.

I just want to fuck hard, though I'm holding back from the full force of what I could deliver, holding on by a fragile string of self-control I am afraid is about to break. That's when her eyes close, her mouth opens, and her arms tighten around me, as if they can get any tighter, and she lets out a cry that's music to my ears.

The throbbing in my balls detonates through my cock, and I'm out of my mind, convulsing, groaning, being reborn, and knowing I'll remember her even if she forgets me tomorrow.

CHAPTER SIXTY-NINE

Charleigh

How is this supposed to work?

Now I have to fake being a virgin? Because I sure as hell am not one anymore.

Vadik told me not to worry about it when I asked, that there would be a surprise later tonight that I'm not to know about until then.

A surprise. Just what I need.

How about a non-surprise? Something predictable? Something *normal*?

Too much to hope for, no doubt.

What could my surprise be? A going away party, maybe? A gift? Another pretty dress to remember my time at the club by?

Goody.

I won't lie. For some truly fucked up reason,

when someone bids on me and I have to say goodbye to the guys, my heart is going to break.

How can I feel this way about men who are about to ruin my life? Throw me away like I'm nothing?

Who do I hate more? Myself or them?

It's a draw.

I'm grateful I lost my virginity to Vadik, and I'd be lying if I don't admit I liked it.

Actually, loved it.

I'm extra-grateful it won't be taken by some creep who buys me like just another possession. He might not know I'm no longer a virgin—you can't always tell, I read in some internet article—but I'll know and I'll be laughing on the inside, enjoying that he was suckered. That's he's getting screwed even more than I am.

God, I sound like a bitter bitch.

In the club's huge party room, I wait out of sight behind a curtain, trying not to shake. Or vomit. Or pass out. I shift in my high-heeled pumps, where I hid my cash under the inner sole lining. It's not comfortable, but what else about my life is? I don't know how tonight will go down, but if I'm whisked off the moment the auction ends, at least I'll have some money with me. I couldn't fit much in there, but it's something.

The troll Alexei, holding the program that still

claims I'm a virgin, is already in the center front row surrounded by his goons, smiling like a cat about to jump its prey. Even from where I am sneaking a peek, I see sweat running down his temples in the temperate room. His sausage-like fingers push through his greasy hair, and he pops a mint into his mouth, his lips twisted into a rubbery smile.

As if his 'having' me is a foregone conclusion.

Such arrogance.

If this doesn't put me off men for the rest of my life, I don't know what will.

I spot Dimitri, who walks in like he owns the place and because of course, there's instant drama over something he says, which I cannot hear across the room. I can't tell whether the guys are trying to corral him or kick him out altogether. God knows what he's done this time. He's his own worst enemy with his big mouth and clueless entitlement.

"How you feeling?" Kir asks, poking his head behind the screen where I wait, startling the hell out of me.

I want to hit him. But I smile and shimmy in my gold dress. "Wonderful Kir, like any girl who's about to be sold to erase the debts of her father. It's what I've always wanted. The perfect direction for my life. My mother, if she were alive, would be thrilled."

His head snaps back on his shoulders like he's

surprised at my vitriol. Does he really expect something else? Am I supposed to be jumping up and down and squealing like a girl who just made the cheerleading squad?

Fuck him. And fuck his brothers.

I look away, full of disgust in myself, the Alekseevs, all the men at the auction, and the world in general.

Everyone gets a break in life. Everyone except me, that is.

I lose my mother when I'm ten, my dad stops being a parent and can barely even continue to run his little business, I have to raise my younger sister, and then *this*? After I finally believe I have a track to follow that will put my life on a trajectory that I control? I wanted to be a professional woman who wears nice clothes and eats in restaurants every now and then. Hangs out with my BFF, Luci, and even takes occasional vacations to warm places like Florida and California.

How is it that's too much to ask?

Where's *my* fucking break?

"Um, I take it Vadik hasn't spoken to you," he says.

No, he hasn't spoken to me. He fucked me, but he hasn't spoken to me.

I don't bother answering. My scowl says it all.

Kir nods slowly. "Okay. Well, just hang tight. One of us will be right back."

I throw my arms up in the air. "Hanging!" I say as if I'm having fun.

He disappears and I look around the screen again, this time watching Dominika get in on the drama at the back of the room.

Anger wells up in me. Actually, it kind of rolls over me, squashing me like a Mack truck. It oozes out of my pores, through the ends of my hair, and if someone were to even look at me wrong, I think I could kill them with my bare hands. My skin crackles with the strange sensation, and the depth of hate I feel at this moment scares me. I'm trying to shake it off when I hear raised voices. I poke my head around the screen again.

Everyone is still preoccupied with Dimitri—even Alexei is now turned around to watch the fuss—that the club front door is not being watched. Seriously. The bouncer, on his way to restrain Dimitri, has left the door unattended.

Could it really be this easy?

I can run. For god's sake, I can run.

CHAPTER SEVENTY

CHARLEIGH

Something holds me back.

Stupidity is the best way to describe it.

Guilt.

How fucked am I?

I feel guilty about the guys. About leaving them. Letting them down.

But do they feel badly about what they're doing to me? I doubt it.

I take one more look at Alexei's doughy, pock-marked profile, and I know.

I come out from behind the screen and slowly walk across the room, like I have somewhere to go.

Miraculously, no one notices me. No one is paying any attention to the coveted prized possession that I am. Their ace in the hole. Their sure thing.

And then I'm outside. The bright street lights blind me for a second, but I manage to make out a taxi that just dropped off some passengers. They look at me oddly in my gold dress, as if they're not sure whether I'm the actual woman up for auction, or someone working for the club.

I smile at them. "You'd better hurry, gentlemen," I say, gesturing toward the door. "The auction is about to start."

They nod in appreciation and pick up the pace.

"Go," I yell at the cab driver after I slam the door.

He hesitates, glancing at me in the rearview mirror.

"Please. Please. We need to go," I plead.

And bless him, he peels out of the parking lot and takes the first highway exit. I slump down in case anyone catches up, looking for me.

The anger overwhelming me seconds earlier is replaced by terror, terror that I'll be caught at any moment. It won't take the guys long to realize I'm gone.

When they do, how will they feel? Betrayed? Angry? Sad?

Will they feel guilty like I do?

Which is such bullshit.

And if it is, why do I feel like my heart is breaking?

The cabby throws a baseball cap and hoodie over the seat for me. "Here," he says. "Someone left these behind. I was gonna turn them in, but you look like you need 'em." Grungy as they are, I pull them on. I am grateful, wrapped in a momentary layer of safety.

God bless him, as my mother would say.

"Where to, ma'am?" he asks.

I give him an address, and he nods.

Am I finally getting my break?

Find out what happens to Charleigh in the next
Beauty & the Bratva novel,
Brutal Ruin:

ABOUT THE AUTHOR

Dear Reader:

I'm USA TODAY bestselling romance author Mika Lane, and am OBSESSED with bringing you sassy, steamy stories with imperfect heroines and the bad-a*s dudes they bring to their knees. I'll always bring you my signature humor and heat, topped off with a modern-day happily ever after.

My first book ever was *The Day I Ate the Milkyway,* a true fourth-grade masterpiece illustrated with crayons and bound with construction paper and glue. Nowadays, steamy romance gives purpose to my days and nights as I create worlds and characters that tickle the imagination. I live in magical Northern California with my own handsome alpha dude, sometimes known as Mr. Mika Lane, and two devilish cats named Chuck and Murray.

A dual citizen of the United States and Ireland, I have on more than one occasion spent my last dollar on a plane ticket somewhere, and am always planning my next escape. I often try new recipes on unsuspecting friends, search out hiding places to read undisturbed, and sadly kill every houseplant I bring home.

I LOVE to hear from readers when I'm not dreaming up naughty tales to share. Visit my online shop https://mikalaneshop.com/ and say hello https://mikalaneshop.com/pages/meet-mika.

xoxo, Mika